SUDDENLY SHE WAS KISSING
HIM BACK . . .

. . . eager for just one taste of the lips that were so inviting.
Just one more moment in his sheltering arms, to feel his
protection, to feel his warm, comforting embrace, then she
would push him away. Her emotions swirled inside her,
forcing her to recognize their ever-rising power. She
pushed them aside, but they rose again with each murmur
of sweet encouragement from Fletcher's lips. And as his
warm hand caressed the satiny flesh of her shoulder, she
knew her control hung by the barest thread. . . .

A CANDLELIGHT ECSTASY ROMANCE ®

CACTUS ROSE

Margaret Dobson

A CANDLELIGHT ECSTASY ROMANCE®

Published by
Dell Publishing Co., Inc.
1 Dag Hammarskjold Plaza
New York, New York 10017

Dell ® TM 681510, Dell Publishing Co., Inc.

Candlelight Ecstasy Romance®, 1,203,540, is a registered
trademark of Dell Publishing Co., Inc., New York, New York.

ISBN: 0–440–11290–7

Printed in the United States of America

First printing—May 1983

To Our Readers:

We have been delighted with your enthusiastic response to Candlelight Ecstasy Romances®, and we thank you for the interest you have shown in this exciting series.

In the upcoming months we will continue to present the distinctive sensuous love stories you have come to expect only from Ecstasy. We look forward to bringing you many more books from your favorite authors and also the very finest work from new authors of contemporary romantic fiction.

As always, we are striving to present the unique, absorbing love stories that you enjoy most—books that are more than ordinary romance.

Your suggestions and comments are always welcome. Please write to us at the address below.

Sincerely,

The Editors
Candlelight Romances
1 Dag Hammarskjold Plaza
New York, New York 10017

CHAPTER ONE

A graceful hawk circled lazily overhead as Casey Robbins sat behind the wheel of the old Scout and drummed her fingers on the metal dash. The vehicle should have been tuned up before leaving Dallas, she admitted. Now it had died just a mere twenty-five miles from her destination. She examined the forsaken Texas road before her.

God, it was a lonely road. Not even a diesel in sight to relieve the deafening silence. She lifted her ebony hair off her neck, then pushed out her lower lip and blew upward in a feeble attempt to dry the beads of perspiration that clung to her forehead. Twilight had brought no respite from the sweltering heat that threatened to swallow her, although the Gulf of Mexico couldn't be more than ten or fifteen miles away.

She was already more than two hours late, Casey reasoned, and Fletcher would be waiting for her at the ranch. Surely he would realize something had happened. Surely he would come out to help.

Casey stared at the white bolls of a parched cotton field that spread alongside the deserted highway, and allowed the memory of her ex-husband to wash over her. Why would she expect his help? She had tried not to depend on Fletcher for anything from the moment she met him, right up to the day she divorced him two years ago. Knowing from the start how he scorned dependence, she had always pushed herself to be the strong, independent woman she knew he wanted. Fletcher had taught her to be a survivor in any situation. Casey had to admit that that knowledge had come in handy during her travels as a geologist with Barton, Haynes, & Robbins. As the only female member of the team, she'd had to prove her skill and expertise over and over in her few years in the business. Her record for sniffing out oil was impressive but, still, she had faced the look of doubt in the eyes of each new client. Perhaps it was her slight, delicate-looking build that put off prospective clients.

Casey used to sweep her thick black lashes low to hide the emerald anger she knew was in her almond-shaped eyes. Men. It seemed that taking professional women seriously was beyond their scope of understanding. They either cocked their heads in cynicism or leered in lust.

She wrinkled her nose in disapproval at the thought, then quickly raised slender fingers to smooth the soft corrugations. Once Fletcher would have done that for her. His affectionate gesture, along with the amusement in his blue-gray eyes, would have softened her mood. He could always smooth her irritation with one soft smile, one touch of his strong fingers on her wrinkled nose.

He had never doubted her, never patronized her as had other men. Fletcher believed her capable of doing anything she set out to do. Encouragement, faith, and love. That kind of support had been important facets of their relationship. The good parts. He would have been disappointed to know just how much she had wanted to rely on his strength in the days when she was working for her master's degree in Geology.

10

"Texas is a harsh, unyielding country," he had said. "People, women especially, have to be strong enough to *take* whatever they want from it."

Her most ardent champion. Her severest critic, Casey thought with a sigh. Fletcher must have seen himself as her mentor, never allowing her to fail at any goal, never allowing her time to mope or complain. How she would have liked to just lean on him once in a while. But she had never allowed herself that luxury. *That* was weakness: the flaw she knew Fletcher most disdained in a man or a woman—the one, unforgivable flaw that would have cost her Fletcher's love had she allowed her moments of weakness to show. Of course, in the end, she thought bitterly, that love had been lost to her anyway.

With no effort at all she conjured his rugged, Texas-tanned face, framed with windblown blond hair. No matter how he combed it, Fletcher could never tame his unruly hair. Sandy, gold-tipped lashes concealed any emotions he chose not to reveal. A lift of his tawny brows could mean almost anything, from mild surprise—Fletcher was rarely shocked—to soft sarcasm, and he was never cruel.

Casey felt the muscles around her eyes contract as she smiled at the bittersweet memory of him. Even now her mind could see the naked desire in his eyes, his muscular, sun-bronzed torso propped against silken-cased pillows, staring as she slowly undressed. It was almost a game to see who could hold out longest before reaching for the other. Each had enjoyed a share in the victories. Neither had ever lost in the battle of wills.

Oh, he wanted her. That had always been clear. But *needing* her. Had he ever needed her? That's why, after two long, silent years, she had been so shocked to receive his cablegram.

Casey reached for her straw bag and searched through

the jumble inside for the now-frayed piece of paper. She must have read it a hundred times since first holding it in her hands while on assignment in Oman. Now she read it again, not really seeing the words; for those were etched in her mind so deeply that she hardly needed the proof. But the feel of the no-longer-crisp paper against her fingers somehow assured her of the reality of the words: I NEED YOU. FLETCHER.

Again she read the words, aloud this time, pondering all their possible meanings. Why now? And for what purpose? Had he finally realized it wasn't a sacrilege for a man and a woman to depend on each other? Was *that* the reason? She feared it was. She feared it wasn't. In the dim diffusion of sunlight she stared at the paper, a gamut of emotions stirring within her. Faint hope trickled through her only to be confronted by the stronger sense of doubt that erupted from the pit of her stomach.

Did he mean the words, or was this just his way of saying he desired her presence at the ranch in the fewest words possible?

Casey chided herself for all the conjecture. The sooner she found out what was wrong with the Scout, the sooner she'd know Fletcher's real reason for summoning her back. It was exasperatingly clear that she was on her own. Only a few cars had slowed enough for their passengers to peer at her, but none had bothered to stop and offer assistance, although the raised hood of the Scout could leave no doubt of her predicament.

She fumbled in the glove compartment for a flashlight. A few taps against her palm and a flick of the switch brought a stream of light. She picked up each article in the glove compartment and laid it down again, silently taking inventory. A screwdriver, pliers, a pocket knife, a roll of electrical wire, and an ancient candy bar. And the last time that wire had been used was when Fletcher had—

Wait a minute! Hadn't Fletcher hot-wired the Scout once when the points had failed? She would never forget his lecture on keeping her Scout tuned up. Well, she hadn't followed his advice on that subject too closely, but maybe she could remember his temporary solution to the problem.

Her body and mind meshed into high gear as she clutched the wire, screwdriver, and pocket knife and deposited herself confidently on the fender outside. Removing the large round breather, Casey peered at the cylindrical black coil that rested near the fire wall. Slightly surprised and encouraged that the part she needed was actually there, Casey loosened the screw atop the coil, then used the knife to strip the ends of the wire, removing the protective rubber coating. With deft fingers she twisted one end of the copper strand around the screw and retightened it. Stretching the wire across the engine, she wrapped the other end around the positive post of the battery, all the time impervious to the tiny jolts of electricity that flashed from the wire through her fingers. Actually, she smiled at the sparks, for they assured her of success.

Flinging herself onto the seat inside, she depressed the clutch and switched on the key. The instant humming of the engine was sweet music to her ears. How could she ever have considered junking the Scout? It just needed better care, she decided, grinning as she patted the dash. This old heap, six hundred forty acres of land, and the Robbins name were all she had left from her marriage to Fletcher. Casey didn't intend to surrender any of it. She jumped from the Scout with determination, replaced the breather, and lowered the hood.

"Thanks, old girl. I knew you could do it," she said, giving the hood one last affectionate pat before she returned to the wheel and sped toward Fletcher and all the memories that had been pushed to a safe, impregnable fortress inside her. She was in no hurry to dredge them up, either, but something about the summer evening under the canopy of a star-studded Texas sky put her in a melancholy mood.

The last red glow of sunlight had disappeared over the horizon as Casey switched on the headlights and smiled to herself, thinking of the impression most people had of Texas. Many dismissed this huge state as nothing but dry, dusty desert, not fit for any life other than rattlesnakes and cacti. And that was a true impression of some parts. She had often heard the menacing rattle of an angry snake herself and had felt the prick of sharp cactus needles countless times, but there was much more to the Gulf coastal region than that. Fletcher's ranch alone contained a topography ranging from marshes to rich black farmland. Then there were the thick growths of mesquite and rolling grasslands.

She loved every inch of it. The Circle R extended over nearly half a million acres with four divisions in Texas alone, and Fletcher and his father, Mack, had holdings in Australia and North Africa. But Casey knew little about those.

For the better part of her marriage she had confined herself to the headquarters here, just outside Robbinsville. For more than a hundred years the Robbins family had used the land for one of the largest cattle breeding operations in the world. Much of her time was spent with Mack, a delightful companion, while Fletcher traveled to the far ends of the earth to check on his foreign interests. Sometimes Mack had entertained her with stories of his youth as a riverboat pilot on the Mississippi.

The gratitude and affection she felt for her ex-father-in-law suddenly came rushing back to Casey as she swallowed hard to rid herself of the lump in her throat. If not for his constant friendship and understanding, she doubted her marriage to Fletcher would have lasted as long as it had.

She wondered if either Fletcher or Mack had changed in the past two years. Surely not Mack. Casey hoped he would be the same crusty codger she remembered, with his silver-streaked hair and steel-wool beard. He would be nearing retirement age now, but Casey suspected Mack had always been in retirement. No nine-to-five job for him. He worked when there was work to be done and took his relaxation whenever he felt the need, leaving everyone else on the ranch free to do the same.

To a certain extent Fletcher had followed in Mack's footsteps. His attitude of "live and let live as long as the work gets done" carried over to all the people who worked for him. But not to Casey. Somehow he had expected more from his wife. It was never anything she could really get angry about. Just little things that even as she thought about them now seemed petty. Were they enough to end a marriage? They seemed so at the time, but now, as she steered the Scout past the gates of the whitewashed wooden fence that surrounded the ranch, she wondered if all the pressure she had felt two years ago was really enough to blot out all the love and desire she had felt for her husband?

Downshifting to first gear, Casey slowed the Scout as the lights of the sprawling stucco hacienda drew her closer and closer. The knot of apprehension tightened in her stomach. Until now she hadn't allowed herself to think about their first meeting after so long a time apart; hadn't allowed herself to dwell on the fact that he might have changed. But now, now that he was so near, now that she would see his handsome face in less than five minutes, she was afraid. Would he still have the same feelings for her?

Of course not, silly, she thought to herself. She had left

15

him with only a note to tell of her plans to go to Dallas. He sent his attorney to court to represent him, not bothering to appear himself. He *couldn't* feel the same way. Nor could she.

But how would he treat her? It was simple. If he touched her, if he looked into her eyes, she would know her Fletcher again. The thought made her shiver with expectation.

Casey maneuvered the Scout around the circular drive and stopped it before the wide steps that led to the massive front door. Deliberately she emerged and walked around to raise the hood and disconnect the wire from the battery. Silence again surrounded her as she smoothed the pleats of her white cotton slacks and tucked in the tail of her green-and-white print blouse. The sleeves, rolled up to the elbows, showed a few smudges of telltale grime from the engine. Casey grabbed a rag from the Scout and rubbed the spots vigorously, then tossed the cloth back inside.

So much for my looking cool, calm, and collected, she thought, wrinkling her nose and hoping Fletcher wouldn't notice the stains. The intermittent popping of the cooling motor accompanied her to the door, where she knocked quietly, almost hoping no one would hear. The huge door swung open, though, and the familiar round face of Ella, the housekeeper, greeted her across the threshold.

"Mrs. Robbins! How wonderful to see you again." Ella took Casey's arm and pulled her inside.

"Hello, Ella." Casey hugged her old friend. "It's wonderful to see you, too. Sorry I'm so late, but the Scout chose today of all days to be stubborn." She tried to keep her eyes on Ella but couldn't resist a glance toward the living room. No sign of Fletcher. "I hope I haven't inconvenienced anyone."

"*Anyone* is in the study—pacing." Ella's meaningful smile reddened Casey's face and made her heart begin to hammer against her rib cage. "I think he's on the verge of calling out the Texas Rangers."

"Really?" Casey feigned indifference while she made an effort to get control of her breathing. Had Fletcher been worried? And why should that please her so much?

"Shall I tell him you're—"

"No, Ella. Let me . . . surprise him." The thought of being announced to Fletcher was too proper, too impersonal, when she had once been so intimate with him. "You say he's in the study?"

"Yes, it's right—"

"I know." *I know.* Unaware of whether the words were actually spoken or mere thoughts, Casey turned and took a deep breath. She made her way quietly down the hallway, the open double doors at its end compelling and forbidding at the same time. The air that escaped her lungs came in almost fearful rushes and her feet couldn't seem to decide whether to run or tiptoe to the room.

She heard his voice first, a mellow but commanding tone that halted her progress for a moment. *Oh, God, don't let him be with someone. Not now.* Casey moved closer, absorbing the low sounds as a dry, thirsty sponge would water. When she reached the entry the sight of Fletcher's broad back seemed to drain her energy, making her lean against the door. From weakness or habit, it didn't matter. Her heart thumped wildly as she surveyed her ex-husband. He was obviously in the middle of a phone call and just as obviously dressed to go out.

Fletcher's lightweight beige jacket hugged his powerful shoulders—shoulders that had never sagged from fatigue in her recollection, not even after a grueling day of breaking horses or branding cattle. Her gaze was drawn to the hand that held the telephone receiver to his ear—a strong, masterful hand with a gentle touch that could soothe the most skittish Thoroughbred. His other hand raked his

17

thick blond hair before resting on one muscular thigh that draped the edge of his desk.

"I'm sorry I couldn't meet you for dinner," he said. "My ex-wife is usually more punctual. But I promise to make it up to you, Priscilla."

Priscilla. Casey stiffened and jerked away from the door. Fletcher must have heard the motion. When he stood to face Casey, his square jaw tightened to erase the easy smile on his lips. She saw his hand clasp the receiver as though he might crush the instrument in his fist. The blue-gray eyes squinted slightly at the corners and, with their smoldering inspection, melted her melancholy thoughts of a moment ago to a blur in her mind.

Something said at the other end of the line jolted Fletcher back to his conversation. "What? Yes. Yes, I'll be there as soon as I can get free." Fletcher continued to regard Casey with an intense, almost stark scrutiny, his gold-tipped lashes unblinking. She felt her skin grow warm with apprehension. Yet his words to this Priscilla person were calm, teasing. "Yes, my curious cat, I'll make sure that you meet my—guest very soon."

Guest. Guest. Never had the term had such a deflating effect on Casey. All reason told her she had no right to feel the way she did. She *was* a guest, and Fletcher was free to see any woman he chose. But her mind was bereft of logic at the moment. For the past two years she had refused to think of Fletcher with another woman. Leave it to him to make her face the prospect the moment she set foot in his house. A flash of good sense pointed out the absurdity of her thoughts, but only raw emotions guided her as she watched him slowly lower the phone to its cradle and come toward her.

"Hello." A nod accompanied the smooth, low tone of his voice. He stopped within a foot of her, his eyes conveying irritation and maybe—but she couldn't be sure—a hint of relief. "How have you been?"

"Fine. Just . . . fine."

He extended a hand that might have rested on her cheek had she not willed it back to his side. Rebuffed, the hand clenched to a fist, then relaxed. "Well," he said, lifting one brow, "let's go someplace where we can be more comfortable. You must be tired after your drive. Have you had dinner?"

"No, but I'm not hungry." Before he could reach for her arm, Casey turned and with quick steps marched back down the hallway. "Were you going out, Fletcher?" Calling over her shoulder, she surprised herself with the indifference she was able to conjure. "I'm sorry if I've spoiled your evening."

"You haven't." The words were clipped and close to her ear. "My dinner plans were tentative, but I do have to leave as soon as I get you settled."

Casey stopped at the wide entrance to the living room and turned to him, hoping her disappointment wouldn't show through her thin smile. "Priscilla must be very understanding to wait for you like this."

"She is." With only a slight twitch of his clefted chin, but no apology in his silky, low voice, Fletcher smiled. That teasing smile, along with the gentle hand that squeezed her waist, pushed thoughts of Priscilla from Casey's mind. Flooded with the memory of his touch, she quickly turned away again and stepped from his grasp.

The sight of the place in which she had enjoyed so many comfortable evenings with Fletcher and Mack somehow seemed alien to her now. The overstuffed sofa and chairs, the Remingtons that adorned the ivory-colored walls, even the bric-a-brac she had arranged and rearranged so lovingly, were all in the same spots she had assigned them the last time she was there. All except her favorite easy chair. It had been banished to a lonely position outside the perimeter of the cozy grouping, like a child sent to the corner for misbehaving.

A pang of resentment shot through her. She had "held court," as Fletcher had affectionately termed it, from that chair. He had bought it for her at an antique auction, proudly presenting it to her on a chilly December evening. Together they had re-covered the ragged wing chair in soft brown corduroy. The many hours of studying, reading novels, and playing chess with Fletcher drifted back to her. Now the chair stood regally and isolated, reupholstered in china-blue crushed velvet.

She pushed the hurt aside. After all, Fletcher couldn't know the attachment she felt for a mere piece of furniture. She had never told him. There were so many things left unsaid. So many things Fletcher would have dismissed as sentimental claptrap. Casey looked around for the ivory-and-onyx chess set she'd given him one Christmas, but it was nowhere to be seen.

"The place is pretty much the same as you left it, Casey, all except that chair." Fletcher came forward to sensuously run his fingers over the velvet material. "Priscilla suggested I have it re-covered."

"Did she? It looks very nice." She hated herself for her condescending tone. Aware of his watchful gaze, she moved away slightly. "I notice the chess set is missing. Don't you play anymore?"

"Sometimes, with Mack, but he's not nearly the opponent you were. I stuck the set in the sitting room upstairs."

"Was that Priscilla's suggestion, too?"

"It's good to see you again, Casey," he said, pointedly ignoring her question. "We expected you for dinner. Priscilla was quite eager to meet you."

"Was she? Your curious cat is a little pushy, don't you think?" She turned aside, angry with herself for letting her feelings show so quickly. She heard his sigh, then the familiar low chuckle.

"Don't tell me you've developed a streak of jealousy. It's a little late for that, isn't it?"

"You're right." She lifted an eyebrow in defense. "It was merely an observation, that's all."

He scratched the back of his sinewy, tanned neck, then shoved both hands in the pockets of his beige trousers. "Tell me why you were late. Trouble on the road?"

"Yes, the Scout—"

"The Scout?" He stared at the ceiling and shook his head. "Good God, are you still driving that thing? I thought it would be in a scrapyard by now."

"Well, it isn't. It's right outside your door. And it was only a small problem. Nothing I couldn't handle."

"No doubt." He almost sneered the words. "Still, I'd like to know what the problem was."

"The points, I suppose, but as I said, I handled it."

"I'll have the foreman at the machine shop replace them in the morning, unless, of course, you think you can handle that, too."

"No," she said quietly, ignoring his mockery, "I'd be grateful for the help."

"It's settled, then. Casey, it isn't safe for a woman alone at night on the road. I'll make sure the Scout has a thorough going-over. Then maybe this won't happen again." Was there concern in his voice or merely irritation that she was late? Fletcher took a step closer, and she tried not to tense at his nearness. He was close enough to kiss her, and she waited in frantic expectation, half-wishing he would and detesting every bit of the longing inside her. A silent sigh escaped her as he turned and walked to the bar. "Would you like a drink? What'll you have?" he asked, setting out two small glasses.

"Whatever you're having." With deliberate nonchalance she continued to explore the room. "I believe some-one's waiting for you, though."

"Yes, but as you pointed out, she's very understanding. Let's sit down and talk." He nodded toward the sofa as she took the drink he offered, then followed his lead.

"What is this, Fletcher? Whiskey?"

"Straight Kentucky bourbon. The best in the house." He shrugged and smiled. "That's what *I'm* having. I thought you'd be used to it, working with men all the time as you do." He paused as if waiting for her to comment.

"The men I work with don't drink on the job," she said cautiously, sipping the bourbon. The bitter-tasting liquid slid down the back of her throat and filled her insides with fire. Suppressing a cough, she breathed deeply and shivered.

Fletcher moved closer, resting his arm across the back of the sofa. "What about after working hours?"

"I don't see much of them after working hours," she replied defensively. Irritated that she felt defensive at all, Casey drank more of the bourbon. This time it plunged to the pit of her stomach and radiated to all parts of her body, leaving her breathless. She set the glass down, searching her mind for a more neutral subject. Spotting the familiar Seth Thomas clock on the mantel, she com-pared its nine-thirty time with that of the diamond watch on her slender wrist. "I see the antique clock is still trust-worthy."

"Yes." He finished his drink and rose as if bored with the turn of the conversation. "As a matter of fact, I was thinking of giving it to Priscilla for Christmas. She's ad-mired it often and she's been a good friend."

"Oh, of course," Casey said with an offhand shrug that she didn't feel at all. It had only taken months of searching to find just the right clock for the mantel. "Since you

22

didn't offer it to me, I think it only fitting that a *good friend* should have it."

Fletcher turned to her with eyes of glistening steel. Her cheek flinched at the grating sound of his voice. "I gave you what you asked for, Casey. I always have and probably always will."

With quick steps she walked to the open patio doors and looked out at the starry night. "That's no longer necessary, Fletcher. We're divorced now, or have you forgotten?"

"No, I haven't forgotten that. And I haven't forgotten who asked for it." She heard the click of his heels as he walked to her side. "So don't come here licking your wounds, as though you're the injured party."

"Fletcher, I was only joking."

"You'll pardon me if I don't find the subject amusing." He moved away, and she watched him lean against the bar. "What was it you said in your note? Ah, yes, you needed to find yourself. Well, tell me, did the real Casey Robbins ever step forward, or is she still lurking in the shadows, waiting to be discovered?"

"I didn't think I could make you understand."

"We'll never know, because you didn't bother to try." He lifted his tall, powerful body to its full height, then shook his head. "This isn't why I asked you here."

"Why *did* you want me to come?" she asked, drawn to his side.

"I need your help with something. But let me tell you about it when I come back."

She shrugged weakly.

"I'll have one of the men take your bags to your room. Mack should be down in a minute. Meanwhile, Ella will get you something to eat. I'll be back as soon as I can." He stepped closer, catching her unaware as he lifted her

23

chin. "And Casey, it *is* good to have you here again. Don't spoil it by pretending feelings you don't have."

His words confused her. She would have to think about what he had said, discover the meaning, but then his lips, his soft, gentle lips, covered hers, sending her thoughts reeling, willing her to kiss him back, willing her to show some sign of caring. She felt her eyelids flutter ridiculously as she debated in a daze whether she should respond. But his arms went around her, pressing her closer, and her body made the decision without permission. Her hands betrayed her as they reached up to touch, then caress the hard muscles of his broad shoulders. The old pattern came back so easily. The way he molded her body to his. The way her fingers played with the blond hair at the nape of his neck.

She'd been too long without the feel of his enticing lips, too long without the caress of his strong, pleasing hands. But how could it happen so quickly? Her mind ignored the question as she reacquainted herself with the rippling muscles of his arms. She meant to push him away, but her hands stopped to linger in the tangle of golden hair that peeked out from his open collar. Through the thin material of her blouse, her breasts remembered the feel of his hard chest against them and responded with a hardness all their own, sending shivers of alarm rushing to her brain.

Shouldn't she stop him? Not one good reason for resistance came to mind as her lips parted weakly to receive his warm tongue, which teased the corners of her trembling mouth. If there was a reason, she didn't want to know it. She only wanted to remain here in his protective embrace, to savor the feelings she hadn't experienced for the two long years they'd been apart.

Too soon he released her and stepped back, raising an eyebrow as though to emphasize the mocking smile that seemed to harden his mouth into chiseled stone.

"So the old fire is still there, hey, Casey? Has it been on the back burner for all these years, or has someone been fanning the flame?" His words settled on her ears like a thunderclap, then an echo. "Never mind. That's none of my business anymore." She could only stare in bewilderment as he walked away from her empty arms, then looked over his shoulder. "By the way, while I'm gone feel free to rearrange the furniture. As I recall, that was your favorite leisure activity. Rearranging things to suit yourself. You were good at it too, until you took to rearranging our lives." With that, he was gone.

She stood rooted to the spot where he had left her. The warmth of the room seemed to chill with his passing. The words he had murmured hung in the air like the crack of a whip.

It was a mistake to come back here, she thought, sinking onto the easy chair. An impulsive, impetuous mistake. She'd been prepared for whatever feelings, whatever attitude he would display toward her. But bitterness? No, she hadn't expected that. Fletcher wasn't a vindictive man. He took life as it came, rolled with the punches. Of course, any other man might have despised a wife who pinned a parting note to his pillow, then walked out of his life. But not Fletcher. She knew him too well. Casey had never seen anything or anyone push him past the point of mild irritation. It was as though he were trying to put her in her place, tell her she didn't belong anymore. She knew that. She knew it as well as she knew him. The knowledge hurt, and she knew it shouldn't.

Stubbornly she reminded herself that Fletcher was the one who had asked *her* to come. He *needed* her. The words seemed such a ridiculous lie now. Fletcher didn't need her or anyone else. She had abandoned the job in Oman, left Jim Haynes to finish it while she packed up and came running all the way from the Middle East to Fletcher.

Casey had never left a job unfinished before, and she sure wouldn't do it again. Not for Fletcher or any other man, she decided. He had his nerve, kissing her like that, then leaving so abruptly for the company of some other woman. His ego must have been thoroughly satisfied to know that he could still arouse her so easily. Well, that's all it was. An ego trip for him. Sexual attraction, that's all.

She pressed her hands to her quivering mouth as she lifted her gaze to the ceiling. He had made her so nervous, sizing her up all the time, watching her with his dark eyes, which changed with every emotion. Well, she was free to leave at any time. That knowledge comforted her, calmed her shaken nerves. She would hear him out, maybe spend one night, then make a speedy departure in the morning. Yes, that would be best. After all, she hadn't even seen Mack yet.

Casey spied her unfinished drink on the table and clutched it in trembling fingers. Raising it to her lips, she forced the rest of the bourbon down her throat and turned to see Fletcher's father watching her from the patio door.

"Mack!" She set her glass down and walked into his bear hug. "Mack, it's so good to see you." Tears, unbidden, welled in her eyes and rolled down her cheeks. His wiry whiskers tickled her chin, and she laughed at the same time.

"Why the tears, Casey?"

"I'm sorry. I know how you hate them." She reached for her bag and drew out a tissue. Wiping the moisture from her eyes, she smiled. "You haven't changed at all, Mack."

"Hmph! Yes, I have! I lost ten pounds from this gut," he said, patting his midsection. "You didn't even notice."

She laughed again. He could always make her laugh. "Now that you mention it, you *do* look lighter."

"So do you, and I'm not so sure I like it. Come on

26

outside so we can talk," he said gruffly, taking her arm. She let him lead her to the charming wrought-iron table and chairs on the patio, where they sat opposite each other, quietly talking over old times. Casey hungrily devoured the appetizing meal that Ella brought out, then settled back in her chair before glancing at her watch. Fletcher had been gone for more than an hour and a half, and she was beginning to wonder how much longer he would be.

"Did he make you cry, Casey?" Mack's gruff voice had softened to a raspy whisper.

"Who? Fletcher?" She shook her head and lied. "No, Mack. I suppose I was just tired from the drive, and then seeing this place again and Fletcher and you . . . all the memories. It just got to me."

"Hmph! I don't know why he would offer you bourbon when he knows you don't like it."

"Mack! You were listening all the time, weren't you?" She cocked her head accusingly but couldn't suppress a crooked smile.

"You bet I was," he admitted flatly, puffing on a cigar. "You two circled each other like a mongoose and a cobra."

"Was it that bad?"

"Well, there was a time or two when I thought you both had retreated to a mutual corner, then Fletcher came out spitting venom again."

"Yes, one last blow before he returned to the doting Priscilla."

"If you think she's doting, wait until you meet 'Daddy,' as she calls him."

"I can't see any occasion for that," she said with a chuckle, leaning closer. "Don't you think it rather gauche for the ex-wife to meet the future father-in-law before the wedding?" She looked to him to share in the joke but noticed the strain in his Fletcher-like eyes.

"If you're looking to me to deny the prospect of a wedding, I'm afraid I can't oblige you, Casey."

Her heart skipped a beat and she struggled to compose herself. "No, no, Mack. Honestly, I wasn't fishing for information. Priscilla is probably a very nice person, and I have no right to—Oh, look, let's talk about something else." She rose and walked to the wrought-iron railing that surrounded the patio. "She's beautiful, I suppose?"

"And blond," he added morosely.

Casey smiled with extreme forbearance. "Young?" The silence that followed told her all she wanted to know. Well, good luck to Priscilla and anyone else who fell in love with Fletcher. Attracting him was only half the battle. Keeping him was the true test—the test that she herself had failed miserably. Her hands gripped the railing tightly in an effort to drive the memory away. "Mack, do you know why Fletcher wanted to see me?"

"Yes, but talk to him about that, Casey. To tell you the truth, I was surprised you came back. You've always been so touchy about anyone trying to manipulate you."

"Well, his cablegram was so cryptic. I thought something might be wrong. I—"

"Don't pretend with me. You didn't ask any questions when you called to say you'd be arriving today."

"I know," she admitted, running her fingers through her raven hair as she returned to the table. "Now that I'm here I realize it was a stupid move. I shouldn't have come."

"Why?" he asked, an indignant frown on his face.

"Because everything's changed, yet everything's the same."

"Now who's being cryptic? Say what you mean, Casey."

28

"Yes, say what you mean, Casey." The sound of Fletcher's deep voice behind her widened her eyes and quickened her breathing. She looked to Mack for support, but he rose and excused himself.

"I need my beauty rest." Mack patted her shoulder, then leaned closer. "Let me know if you need the snakebite kit."

She shot him a frown before he walked slowly into the house. Watching him go, her heart went out to him. She said nothing until he was out of earshot, then turned to Fletcher.

"He's getting older."

"Aren't we all, but don't let that slow walk fool you. He just wanted to hear as much of our conversation as possible before his self-imposed dismissal. He feels a hell of a lot younger than I do these days."

She had to laugh as she watched Fletcher move to a chair and scratch the back of his head. "What's making you feel so old, Fletcher? Is it business, or is your love life with young Priscilla taking its toll?" She could have slapped herself for letting the words escape.

"As a matter of fact, she's two years older than you. Perhaps she just *looks* younger."

"Forget I said that." Her hands erased the words from the air. "You make me feel like such a shrew."

"Don't blame me for the way you behave, Casey. Aren't you the master of your emotions?" A subtle smile spread across his lips, and this time she wanted to slap *him*.

"Of course I am," she insisted. "For instance, right now I feel like breaking this table over your head but, as you can see, I'm restraining myself. Don't push your luck, though."

He laughed until tears came to his eyes. To see him laughing again cut to the very core of her emotions, even though he was laughing at her. She turned away so he

29

couldn't see the love in her eyes. Before she could examine her feelings closely, Fletcher was at her side.

"I've missed you, Casey. You could always make me laugh."

Disappointment dulled her brain and she bit her lower lip and faced him. "Now that I've attained my highest goal in life, why don't you tell me why you sent for me."

The smile on his rugged face disappeared and his bright eyes turned cloudy with gray. His arms folded across his chest as he planted his feet slightly apart. Even in this stubborn stance she couldn't think of him as cold and unbending, no matter how much she wanted to. His very nearness warmed her, drew her closer. It took all her effort to stay away. "It's really very simple," he said. "I know there's oil on my land and I want you to find it."

So that was it, Casey thought with an inward sigh. There was nothing personal involved in Fletcher's summons. Nothing to hint that he might have changed. Absolutely nothing.

CHAPTER TWO

Casey's tired thoughts as well as her exhausted body tossed and turned until the bedclothes finally slipped to the plush salmon carpet in a tangled heap. She switched on the bedside lamp and stood to adjust the silky blue nightgown that had twisted around her well-shaped thighs. As the hem of the material dropped to the floor to hug her body in soft folds, she flung the spread back to the highposter, then settled herself against propped pillows. Tired as she was, she couldn't sleep until her thoughts were sorted out.

Fletcher had given her the bare facts. That's all. He wanted to hire her services in the search for oil on his property. He wanted to get started as soon as she could manage it. He wanted this, he wanted that. Well, she wanted more information. Fletcher was so businesslike, so impersonal, through the whole conversation.

There were many questions she had wanted to ask. Questions she wouldn't have dared to ask any other client, but Fletcher was her ex-husband. Why couldn't she ask him?

It was simple, she told herself with a frown. *Because* he

was her ex-husband, she had no claims, no rights where he was involved anymore. She had no right to ask why he decided to drill for oil on land that had been used exclusively for cattle for well over a hundred years. She couldn't ask why he would risk hundreds of thousands of dollars on a "wildcat" well when his cattle had always been a sure bet. Most of all, she couldn't ask why he had asked *her* to work on the project. There were plenty of good geologists in Texas, some of them in Corpus Christi, not thirty miles away. Instead, he sent a message to the edge of the Rub' al-Khali desert region, halfway around the world, and she had dropped everything to answer his summons.

Well, she wasn't about to be so impulsive this time. That wasn't her style anymore. Now she was on her toes, ready for anything. She needed time to think about his offer and told him as much. He seemed unconcerned about any doubts she might have. Fletcher invited her to stay a few days and relax, get to know the ranch again, then make her decision.

On the surface, that seemed a good idea. A few days here sounded very attractive. She could go for delicious swims in the pool, ride the range with Mack again, and maybe even indulge herself in a shopping spree in Corpus.

Casey sighed, remembering her noncommittal attitude. She had murmured something about having to check with her partners before she could agree to taking on the project. Although she knew there was nothing pressing. Ross and Jim had been after her for months to take some time off. The other two thirds of the firm wouldn't be happy to know she would be spending her vacation working, if indeed she decided to accept Fletcher's offer.

Gathering her knees to her chest, she wrapped her arms around her smooth calves, then wriggled her toes impatiently. If she stayed, what would happen? Could she handle this job as impersonally as all the others? There would be so much money at stake. Fletcher's money. She had worked many times for huge oil companies in their search for new sources of crude. They knew the pitfalls and could absorb the losses, but Fletcher was a cattleman. What did he know of test drilling and what it took to find oil? After all, a geologist couldn't guarantee that the crude would be there. When all was said and done, after the tests were made and the samples studied, she could only point to the spot where it *might* be found. The rest was up to the drilling crew and sheer luck.

Although her skill had brought her good luck so far, she couldn't guarantee Fletcher any profitable results. Was he aware he could spend all that money only to come up with a dry well, perhaps several dry wells?

Yawning lazily, she reached for her thin robe and sank her feet into the luxurious carpet. Slipping into the silk covering, she lifted her long hair free of the collar and padded into the sitting room that separated her bedroom from Fletcher's. His door was closed, but the memories of their time together seemed to emanate through the walls to penetrate her restless thoughts, leaving them more scattered than ever.

She smiled as she walked to the window and looked out at the black night dotted with stars. She thought how surprised her colleagues and employees would be if they knew the memories she kept locked in her heart.

Casey was well aware of her reputation in the petroleum world. What was it they called her? Cactus Rose. Yes, that was it. Of course, no one had ever been crass enough to call her that face-to-face, but word had gotten around that she was a woman impervious to even the smoothest approach. She had never allowed flirting, not even the light, innocent kind to creep into her work. There were never sexual overtones of any kind in her dealings with the drilling crews or other geologists, not even the men who hired her services. Word had spread fast that the men could look all they wanted, but to touch her would result in a swift and sharp rebuff, guaranteed to draw blood from even the most tough-skinned egos. She wasn't pleased with the unflattering term but accepted it as an inevitable result of her determination to be a respected member of her profession. Besides, no man had ever come close to sparking the desire that Fletcher had so easily kindled within her.

The many treasured nights she had spent in his arms came flooding back to her. Those were the only times she really felt close to him. Fletcher rarely revealed to anyone his innermost thoughts. Outside their sexual relationship, it was as though she didn't belong. Casey asked few questions about the running of the ranch, and Fletcher had expressed little interest in her work. Although a member of the bar, he had turned away from law, preferring to bury himself in ranch affairs. She had done her best to become the woman she thought he wanted—a wife with a career, friends, a life independent of his. Fletcher was so competent that she felt guilty, inadequate, offering anything less. But she had failed. Her deep-seated fear that she wouldn't be able to hold the interest of such a dynamic man had gradually become a reality. The truth became undeniable the night Fletcher came home from a trip to find her in the arms of Steve Howard, a family friend.

Casey wandered to the back of the sofa to stroke the soft, shiny material with searching fingers. Hugging a throw pillow to her chest, she thought how innocent the whole thing had been. Dr. Howard had merely dropped by to tell her that she was in perfect health, that there was no reason she couldn't have the children she had wanted for the two years of their marriage. Fletcher hadn't known the worry she had experienced, wondering if she would ever become pregnant. She had never confided this secret fear to him, half-afraid that he would view her need for consolation and support as sheer feminine weakness. Of course, later she saw how wrong she had been to remain silent; it was something they should have talked openly about and faced together.

As it happened, when Steve Howard told her the news she had so desperately wanted to hear, she had thrown her arms around his neck in sheer relief and gratitude. The minute Steve was gone, of course, she hastened to explain under Fletcher's cool, assessing stare. But he wanted no explanation.

"Spare me the details, Casey," he had said. "Just fix me a drink while I shower. I'd like to turn in early tonight."

When she tried again to explain as she lay beside him in bed, she could feel his cool indifference closing her out, pushing her aside.

"Casey, you are, after all, your own person, free to do as you please." He spoke in an even tone, his voice emotionless. "I only ask that you be a little more discreet," he added a moment later.

Casey tossed the pillow back to the sofa and turned away. Even now she remembered his casual kiss before he rolled onto his side and fell asleep, but she wasn't able to share his blasé attitude.

To her love meant faith, trust, and fidelity. When that bond was broken, what was left? How empty and disillusioned she had felt to learn that it wasn't so for Fletcher. She had felt so incredibly cold, as if she were lying next to a stranger. She had loved Fletcher, but was that enough? If Fletcher didn't care if she had an occasional affair, then what did he care about?

That night had been the beginning of the end for Casey. The answer to her question became painfully clear as, with each passing day, she began to believe that she had to get away, to reassess her marriage and her values. She had

35

gone to Dallas first and worked on her own for a time before joining the firm of Barton, Haynes, & Robbins as a full partner. Never fully understanding the complexity of her relationship to Fletcher, she had eventually pushed it to the back of her mind, promising herself that with time she could examine it with more objectivity.

She had made a new life for herself, a damn good one.

So why was she standing here now, forcing herself to look back at the painful memories? She couldn't answer that. Casey only knew that she had organized her life carefully, keeping each area separate, rarely seeing the need to scrutinize the more intimate feelings that she'd tucked in the cubbyholes of her mind. Mostly she thought about business, and business never spilled over into her personal life. Until now.

That's what she'd be doing if she took this job. Mixing business with personal affairs. Could she possibly be indifferent to a man she'd been so deeply in love with? No, not indifferent. But surely she had enough control over herself to resist any advances he might make, if he made any. She'd had two years to practice. Yes, she could do it—if she wanted to.

Casey jumped at the sound of a doorknob turning. Fletcher stood in the doorway, his face bathed in the soft glow of moonlight spilling through the open window. Her heart leaped at the sight of his tousled hair, his tanned, muscular chest. He wore only the bottoms of black silk pajamas, his hand resting easily on the hard flesh above a loose-fitting waistband. With each step he took toward her, she was reminded of his penchant for—his insistence on—comfortable clothing. She watched the pajamas slip of their own volition a fraction lower on his hips. Casey looked away, confused by the guilt that made her do so.

It was as though she had no right to the pleasure of looking at this man now. Why should she care? She knew

Fletcher certainly didn't. Besides, his confidence alone would probably save his pants from dropping to the floor if he didn't want them there. She recognized the flip conjecture as an attempt to curb her racing pulse. But the recollection that Fletcher had most often worn nothing at all in this room, and the knowledge that she hadn't either, canceled out her efforts, especially when he stood near to her—as he did now.

"Can't you sleep, Casey?"

"I was just about to try again. Sorry I woke you."

"You didn't. I couldn't sleep, either. It's not easy, knowing you're in the house but not in my bed." His gaze raked her body, making her skin grow warm against the material of her gown. "Is that what's keeping you awake, too?"

"No, Fletcher, it isn't." Irritated that he had come so close to the truth, she moved toward her bedroom. "I think I can sleep now." His hand stopped her with gentle, warm pressure on her arm.

"Wait. You must have something on your mind that won't let you sleep. Would you like a drink or some warm milk, maybe?" he asked, leading her to the sofa.

"No, but I would like some answers."

"About what?" He pulled her down beside him.

"This oil business. The whys and the wherefores." Aware that his arm rested on the back of the sofa, she remained perched on the edge of the seat. "For instance, I know that Mack has always been against the idea of drilling for oil on the Circle R."

"That's true. He didn't want any interference with cattle operations, and I've always deferred to his wishes on that matter; but we've managed to find someone who's willing to cooperate with us and work around the cattle. They're still our prime consideration."

"But Fletcher, it takes a lot of money just to drill one

37

well." She turned to him to make sure he understood what she was saying. He stared back at her, a slight smile touching his lips.

"I'm not totally ignorant on the subject. You can't live in Texas and not know something about oil, Casey, but thanks for the concern. And don't sell yourself short." He pulled her against the back of the sofa. "I have complete faith in you. I know the risks involved, but I also know you'll do the best job possible. You won't fail me in that area."

That was exactly what she feared. Failing Fletcher. She had left him, afraid she couldn't live up to his ideal. Afraid she couldn't be the person he insisted she was capable of becoming, not knowing if she even wanted to be. Now she felt herself sinking back into the old trap of wanting desperately to please Fletcher, instead of herself.

When she felt his warm breath on her cheek, thoughts of another trap sped through her. He nibbled tenderly, maddeningly on her ear. Drawing away, she frowned. "Don't, Fletcher. This is all wrong."

"It all seems right to me," he said, stroking the back of her neck. Immediately she recognized a familiar prelude to more passionate moments with Fletcher. She let out a soft cry of protest and started to rise, but he turned her face to him, kissing her in a slow, teasing manner.

"Fletcher, don't—do this to me. We have things to talk about. We have to—"

"Talk is the last thing I want right now." He kissed her eyelids, then the tip of her nose. His lips lingered at the corner of her mouth, daring her to respond. "You're just as beautiful now as you were when I met you. More beautiful, I think, Casey."

"I'm not the same. We're not married anymore."

He moaned softly, pulling her closer. "No piece of paper ever kept us apart before we were married. Why

38

should it now?" His expert hands stroked her waist, brushing the sides of her breasts with each up and down movement.

She could hardly believe her own quiescence. She did nothing except stare into his eyes, knowing she should say something, do something. But she didn't. And she wasn't shocked by Fletcher's audacity. She'd seen that before. Besides, shock had no place among the sensations her body, her mind, enjoyed at the moment. It was pure, delicious pleasure, given by a man who knew how. God, how was he always able to do this to her? How did he always know when to do it?

It was slow, sweet torture as his lips continued to plant tender kisses on her shoulder, then her neck, on up to her tingling ear, then returned to her mouth with a growing urgency. She parted her lips, longing to feel the warmth of his tongue.

As if lying in wait for the invitation, his tongue slowly entered to explore the beginning of her anticipation. Her trembling fingers stroked the firm line of his jaw, then reached around to the comfortable spot at the back of his neck to entwine his blond hair. Mmmm, hair that felt like fine cornsilk, soothing her doubts, then bringing them back, blending all her discordant thoughts into one strong desire to have him love her again.

The kiss she returned was fraught with confused retreats and advances. If she could have just *one* taste of the lips that were so inviting. Just *one* moment in his sheltering arms, to feel his protection, to feel his warm, comforting embrace, then she would push him away. Her emotions swirled inside her, forcing her to recognize their ever-rising power. She pushed them aside, but they rose again with each murmur of sweet encouragement from Fletcher.

"You taste so good. You feel so good." He kissed her

again, this time letting his tongue seduce her mouth with a sensuous glide over her lower lip until it quivered with want of him.

When he finally took possession, her pent-up desire spilled over its confines. She pressed against him, her lips clinging, giving . . . her tongue searching, taking.

With a masterful hand he stretched the yielding fabric of her gown across her breast. Without looking down, she knew the outline of a taut nipple would be unmistakable. His searing fingers drew rings of fire around the outward curve of the sensitive swelling. As the circles became smaller, spiraling to the center, the tiny swirls of his thumb produced a tormenting throb. It was so intense, so near the surface, that she ached with a need to have his mouth on her breast.

When his gaze eased up to hers, there was almost a predatory hunger in his eyes. "Tell me what you want, Casey. Right now . . . at this moment." His fingers continued with easy strokes, circling her breast, waiting.

She looked away from the question in his eyes and on his lips. God, she couldn't tell him. She'd never had to before. And she wouldn't now. Words would commit her to everything that might happen in the next few minutes. There would be no turning back, no denial later, no claim that he had misunderstood her actions. He was demanding a conscious, rational decision on her part—one that she was in no position to give.

Moving from the circle of his arms, she rose with weak knees, putting distance between herself and the man who threatened to crumble every barrier she had constructed. "Fletcher, if this is going to happen every time we're alone, I won't be able to stay," she said breathlessly, wishing her voice didn't sound so weak. "I think it would be better to keep things on a strictly business basis. After all, neither of us is the same as we once were."

"You keep saying that, Casey, and you could be right. It remains to be seen, but some things never change . . . *do* they? I still want you as much as I ever did." He came to her side and reached out, grasping her hand. When she resisted, he held her hand firmly. Raising it to his lips, he kissed her slender fingers. "How do you keep such long, beautiful nails with the kind of work you do?" He molded her palm to his rugged, sculptured face.

Again his touch, the intimate gesture, threatened to dissolve her control. With a wrenching effort she pulled away. "Fletcher, be serious. If I do agree to stay, you'll have to promise—"

"Don't even ask." The provocative tone would have been warning enough, but Fletcher emphasized the words with an arch of one tawny brow. "If you were about to say I'll have to leave you alone, forget it. I could promise you that and every planet in the solar system, but it wouldn't mean a damn thing."

He said it so smugly, so self-assuredly, that anger crackled inside her. "Then you just lost yourself a geologist." The shake of her long hair formed a dusky cloud of defiance as she walked to the door of the guest room. When she reached for the knob, Fletcher's derisive chuckle reached her ears.

"Well, Priscilla said you'd run like a scared rabbit. She said you wouldn't be able to face me and the memory of our marriage."

"What's she got to do with this?" Casey snapped. Turning to him, she lifted her chin and forced back the tide of resentment within her.

"She and her father are my partners," he said with a shrug, then a sideways glance. "They wanted a geologist from Corpus. Henry Ames said a woman would be too unreliable, too unsettling. He didn't think a woman could

41

work with his drilling crew without mucking up the operation. Mack came to your defense, of course."

She had to smile at that. Leave it to Mack to toot her horn whenever she wasn't around to do it herself. "What did Mack say, Fletcher?"

"He got rather testy with them. Told Henry that you were the person for the job, and if Henry didn't want you, then we could all count him out of the deal. For a while there I thought he might ask Priscilla to step outside." His dark eyes twinkled as he conveyed that bit of information.

She laughed outright. In her mind's eye she could see Mack, a big bear of a man, making threats against the likes of Priscilla. Casey loved him all the more for his words on her behalf.

"What about you, Fletcher? Since you all seem to have taken a poll, what was your opinion?"

He sighed as one hand went to the back of his neck, then dropped to his side. "I've never doubted your ability as a geologist or as a woman. Despite your reservations, I hope you'll stick around a few days, like you said you would, then sign a contract to stay until we hit pay dirt. But if you can't do that, I'll understand."

"Would you, Fletcher? I wonder. . . ." She saw the look in his eyes, a look she had never seen before and couldn't comprehend.

"You might be surprised at the things I understand—now." His gaze was riveted to hers for what seemed like aeons. It was as though her life with him flashed before her eyes, as though she were drowning. Finally she forced herself to look away.

"Well, I think I can sleep now. I'll give you my answer tomorrow, Fletcher. Good night."

As she slipped into bed Casey knew she had just been beautifully manipulated by an expert. Still, she had to admire his ability. Fletcher hadn't lost his touch at all. He still reigned supreme in subtly challenging her, daring her to come out swinging. He knew all the right things to say, all the right buttons to push, mentioning Priscilla, whom he knew she could easily despise, then smoothly bringing Henry Ames into the picture to question her ability as a geologist. He topped it all off with a vote of confidence from Mack, whipped cream to stroke her ego and soothe her rattled nerves. His own words had been the crowning touch. He had played this game before. She knew exactly what he had tried to do, and Casey smiled to herself as she snuggled among the bedclothes, for she also knew that sometime during the next few days she would tell him, reluctantly, of course, that she would take the job.

CHAPTER THREE

Shivering from the cold water, Casey lifted herself from the pool and reached for a large fluffy towel to dry her face. The rest of her body glistened as she molded herself to the form of the chaise longue, then pushed fashionable sunglasses to rest on the bridge of her nose.

She was still in good shape, she reminded herself with a satisfied smile. Five laps in Fletcher's pool hadn't tired her at all, but Casey knew she should take it slow at first. There hadn't been time or opportunity for such vigorous exercise in the last few years. Not like the old days, when she had greeted each sunny morning with a relaxing, but exhilarating swim. Her muscles had responded beautifully after the initial shock of such strenuous movement. Those in her thighs still trembled in short spasms as if clamoring for more, but Casey gave them one good stretch and a promise before she rolled onto her stomach to let her back soak up the warm sunshine.

She thought how lucky she was that her yellow tank suit still fit after all this time. Neglecting to bring her new suit, Casey had resigned herself to a swimless morning, when eager-to-please Ella whisked the old yellow suit from a cardboard box in the attic. Casey had spent the better part of the morning going through the other long-forgotten cartons of odds and ends with Ella as they reminisced, exchanging lighthearted memories as well as those tinged with sadness. She instructed Ella to offer the old dresses to a local thrift shop, but she pocketed the ivory pendant and matching earrings that lay folded away in faded tissue paper.

Now, as she lay beside the pool, Casey draped her long hair over one shoulder and fingered the gold chain that held the ivory ankh. The ancient Egyptian symbol for life, she thought with a sigh. Fletcher had given the exquisite pieces to her upon his return from a trip to Africa, and she had cherished them. She still did and couldn't think how she had forgotten the jewelry in her haste to leave so long ago.

Hmmm. Mere trinkets to Fletcher, no doubt, but to me they are a symbol of our life together, mine and Fletcher's.

Fortunately Ella had boxed up all her belongings, perhaps knowing that someday Casey would return for them. Ella was like that; the intuitive sort who usually relied on basic feelings to guide her. Not like herself, Casey thought with a mental shrug. She had schooled herself to analytical thinking during the past few years. Intuition and deep, dramatic feelings had no place in her life now, certainly not in her work. She took pride in her objectivity, not being subject to fanciful daydreaming. Not until yesterday, anyway. Seeing Fletcher again had released a flood tide of feelings that she quickly dammed up again before the inundation overtook her.

Casey's mouth twisted in disgust. That very morning had brought another crack in the dam. Eager to share the memory of the ankh with Fletcher, she had skipped downstairs in search of him. She had found him, all right—in the company of a delicate-looking blonde with blue saucerlike eyes, long dark lashes, and a homebaked pie in each of her finely shaped hands. Even before Fletcher did the honors, then stepped back to watch the show, Casey sensed the woman with the millimeter waist could be none other than Priscilla Ames. The perfect little homemaker, she thought dryly, then lifted her brows in guilt.

It was unfair and probably more than a little catty to think of the woman in that way. But Casey wasn't in the mood to be charitable. Perhaps the pies had done it—all-American apple, no less. And it had taken only a few minutes to discover that Priscilla was devoted to Fletcher, that she leaned on him and looked to him for advice and direction. And he *let* her.

When the voices of Fletcher and Priscilla drifted to the pool area, Casey closed her eyes and willed her muscles to relax. Since she had already been a party to Priscilla's aimless chattering once that morning, she considered that another encounter would constitute overkill. She kept her eyes closed as the voices came closer.

"Fletcher, I just don't know if I'll ever learn the gears on that Porsche," Priscilla wailed. "I guess I should've chosen one with an automatic transmission, but that car just seemed to call out to me to take it home."

"Don't worry. It's really very simple once you learn the sequence." Fletcher's calm reassurance floated to Casey's ears. "I'm sure you'll get the hang of it after a few more lessons. As your teacher, I think you're a very quick study."

I'll bet. Casey cocked an eyebrow, then quickly lowered it, thankful she was wearing the sunglasses.

"Oh, you've been so helpful, Fletcher, and so patient," Priscilla went on in a lilting voice of gratitude. "Casey, you just don't know what a—Casey?"

"Uh, I think she's asleep, Priscilla," Fletcher said in a

slightly lower voice. "She must still be tired from her trip yesterday."

"You know, I just don't know how she does it, taking off by herself like that. I'm not the type. Daddy would just die if I started out on a trip alone, without some kind of—well, male protection."

Oh, brother, Casey thought with a clenched jaw. Was there no end to this woman's drivel?

"I don't think Casey minds," Fletcher said. "She's a match for any trouble that might come along. In fact, I wouldn't be at all surprised if she *started* the trouble."

Amidst Priscilla's smothered giggles, Casey seethed. What did he mean by that?

"Well, I'm late for my pottery class. Are you sure you won't come with me?" Priscilla's tone was beseeching. "You might enjoy the class. And I could certainly use your muscles to carry that box of supplies."

God, what a—what a— Casey couldn't think what.

"There's nothing I'd like more, Priscilla, but I have that appointment in town. Remember? Anyway, I'll meet you for lunch as we planned. Somehow I don't think pottery is my thing. I'm just not that creative."

If *she* had ever given him an invitation like that to a pottery class, Casey mused, Fletcher would've laughed right in her face. He would have teased her unmercifully. But he wasn't laughing at Priscilla, she reminded herself. What had happened to him?

"Okay, Fletcher." Priscilla sighed. "I'll have to be content with whatever time you give me."

Casey thought she heard a kiss before Priscilla's light steps sounded on the concrete, then eventually faded. She waited for Fletcher's footsteps and a safe span of time to pass until she could open her eyes and relax her jaw. If she hadn't heard it with her own ears, Casey would never have believed Fletcher could be so patronizing. Was it an act? No, she decided. He actually seemed serious.

Suddenly she flinched as she felt his finger sliding the length of her nose, smoothing the wrinkles.

"Casey, if you didn't like the conversation, why didn't you get up and leave?"

"What? And miss that touching scene? Not on your life." Casey shifted onto her back and tried desperately to hide her chagrin. Raising her sunglasses, she peered at him. Fletcher peered back, thoroughly enjoying her discomfort, judging by the slight lift of his brows and the rigid set of his mouth. Remembering that Fletcher had never once been intimidated by her icy stares, Casey lowered the glasses onto her nose again. "I have to admit it was a class act, though."

"It wasn't an act, Casey," he gently chided. "Priscilla just isn't as self-sufficient as you are. You never could tolerate frailty." He stood there above her in his vested blue suit, looking so handsome. His blond hair was combed back, and she had the sudden urge to reach up and restore it to its natural unruly, windblown look—the Fletcher she'd always known. He never used to wear three-piece suits. The thought had come out of the blue, and she dismissed it, returning to the matter at hand.

"I can sympathize with human frailty as well as the next person. It's the phony, clinging vine act I can't seem to stomach."

"Well, you should've made your feelings known instead of lying there, pretending to be asleep." A smile threatened to soften his mouth, but he must have changed his mind, for his lips remained hard as the concrete to which she shifted her gaze.

"I didn't feel it was my place to get involved," she said with as much dignity as she could muster.

48

"No, you never did make the effort—whether it was your place, or otherwise."

"That's not fair," she shouted. "If you're trying to—" She stopped short to lower her voice. "If you're trying to bait me into an argument, forget it." She shifted on the lounger. "I'm older now and I don't bite so easily. Now, the point I was trying to make is that I thought you liked your women independent. That's all." She smiled thinly to punctuate her determination to avoid an argument, but her jaws locked together again.

"Well, I guess my tastes have changed. Dependent women are a lot safer. You independent types are too hard to hang on to."

"That wasn't the reason I left and you know it." Why did he have to go on in that calm, smooth voice when she was getting so irritated?

"No, I confess I never knew the *real* reason. Steve Howard, perhaps?"

"Of course not!" She rose and faced him, hoping her heightened position would help quell her growing anger. "Let's just say that you never offered to carry *my* pottery supplies."

"Oh, that's a good reason." A confused smile spread over his face. "I hope that has a double meaning because, frankly, I'm at a loss."

The heat rose to her cheeks at his smug manner. "If you give it some thought, I'm sure you'll understand."

"Some other time. Look, I don't want to neglect my duties as a host. What can I do to entertain you today?"

"Nothing." She sank back onto the chaise longue and glared into his steel-gray eyes. "I'm perfectly capable of entertaining myself. I plan to stay here awhile longer, then maybe go into town this afternoon for a new straw hat. Is that little western shop still on the corner of Fourteenth and Madison?"

"Yes. Well, if you don't want to have lunch with me and Priscilla, I guess I'll leave you in your own capable hands."

"Oh, Fletcher, please come with me," she said in a Priscilla-like voice. "You know how heavy those hatboxes are." Her eyelashes fluttered demurely as she turned her face and curved one bare shoulder up to meet her cheek.

"No, thanks. I never could stomach the sight of a woman turned green with envy." He turned to leave.

"Oh, no, you don't!" She jumped from the lounger and grabbed his arm. "You're not leaving on that nasty note. Come on, Fletcher. Stay here and fight like a man." Her chest heaved with fury as he merely stared at the white knuckles of her hand on his powerful bicep.

"You don't really want that, Casey. If you don't watch it, you'll be bruising your attractive little tush on the cement before you could bat those charming lashes at me again."

"Okay, let's have it out right now." Cockily lifting her chin, she couldn't help baiting him. "Come on. I want to hear it all. That's why you've brought me here after all, isn't it? Tell me all about how you've waited two years to get even."

He only stood, crossing his arms and shaking his head slowly. "Very nicely said, Casey, but don't transfer *your* feelings to my shoulders. I'll be glad to quietly discuss our marriage and all the gruesome details if you'll keep your voice down. I'm sure Mack would love to hear this."

"I won't keep my voice down!" Her fists, still clenched, dropped to her sides. "When people get angry they raise their voices. That's one of the ground rules."

"I should've known you'd have rules for arguing."

"Well, I do and I'll thank you to abide by them."

"Right," he said in a deceptively even tone. "But first, I think you should cool off, Casey." Without ceremony he

50

picked her up and dumped her into the icy water. Her eyes widened in shock and she felt the chill cut through her body. Raven hair fanned about her shoulders as she surfaced, gasping, sputtering, and bent on revenge.

"That's the way, Fletcher," she taunted as he walked away. "When in doubt, try drowning your opponent!" That monster! How could he have done such a hateful thing? He had never treated her like that!

"Don't stay out here too long, Casey," he called over his shoulder. "You know how easily you burn."

"Go to hell!" she muttered as he disappeared around the side of the house. Casey turned away, trembling as she clung to the edge of the pool and cleared her eyes of water with a wet hand.

What had he done to make her so angry? A quick scan of her memory brought no logical answer as she blinked in confusion. Surely he must have said something, must have done something to upset her so. But what? She closed her eyes, her thoughts still spinning.

Fletcher had told Priscilla he wasn't a creative person, but Casey knew that was a lie. He had made her everything she was today. She could have been a block of clay on a potter's wheel, waiting for someone to come along and mold her, give shape to her life. Fletcher had been that someone. Whenever he wasn't pleased with his efforts, the clay went back to the wheel, reshaped, remolded, until the results satisfied him.

For all the bravado, all the confidence she had shown in herself during their first meetings at college, Casey had actually been alone and afraid. She could admit that to herself, at least, now that she had changed. She had been floundering on her own when Fletcher had taken her in, married her, taught her to survive in a sometimes cold world, then pushed her out into the very world from which he had plucked her. But he had somehow refused to go *with* her.

If anyone had asked her to explain the last few minutes, she would have been hard pressed to offer any rational account. What had begun as gentle jibes suddenly developed into scathing comments, seething accusations. And through it all Fletcher had remained so confident, so cool, and, oh, so arrogant.

With a sigh of regret at her childish behavior, Casey let go of the rough concrete edge and shifted to float on her back. The water was like a soothing cushion of warmth beneath her as she drifted on its shimmering surface. Thoughts of Fletcher rippled through her mind and slowly became congruent with the gentle undulating of her body. It was almost like dancing with him. A shiver tingled her shoulders as she remembered the first few months of her married life. Parties that lasted until dawn —or so she'd been told. She and Fletcher never stayed too late, and their dances were only for each other. With his arms around her, holding her close, he had teased her mercilessly with ideas of what he would do to her later when they were alone. And if by chance she was separated from him by a guest who wanted to talk business, she knew by the strain in his watchful, impatient eyes that Fletcher wouldn't stay away long. He would come back to her, hold her more tightly than before, make her want him with tender, exciting caresses. Then, when he reached the limit of his endurance, he would give her a signal— always a nibble on her ear—and nudge her toward the hostess to offer the prearranged excuse for leaving early. It was always the same one: that he and Casey didn't want to leave Mack at home alone too long.

Casey smiled, remembering the last time Fletcher had used that excuse. A tactful hostess had refrained from pointing out that Mack was on the dance floor, accosting every unattached female in sight.

It was wonderful . . . so wonderful. Until they began to grow apart. Before long studying became the central point of her life. Between that and Fletcher's work, there didn't seem time enough for parties and trips and entire days spent concentrating on each other. Fletcher began leaving her alone, sometimes for business, sometimes for pleasure. But the reasons didn't matter. She had missed him all the same.

Springing herself from the water, Casey let out a deep breath and sank onto the chaise longue. With a heavy head she stretched the length of the flowered cushions and rested an equally heavy arm across her eyes.

Was Fletcher right? Was it her own bitterness, her own resentment at not being with him for two years that had triggered the volatile explosion? Was that it?

No, she told herself sternly, rolling onto her stomach. She had adjusted to that. She *knew* she had. Fletcher's absence had left a terrible void in her life but, in time, she had filled it with work, casual friends, a fairly full social life, or at least as much as she could tolerate. So why the short fuse?

Priscilla. It must have been Priscilla, Casey told herself drowsily. *Yes, that's the only explanation.* Yawning, she decided to rest a minute, then have a long, hard think about Priscilla . . . and how weak . . .

Casey closed her eyes and slept.

Vaguely aware of stinging pain, Casey lifted her head and squinted her eyes, level with Fletcher's perturbed gaze.

"Casey, have you been out here all this time?" he asked, kneeling beside her.

"I suppose I have." She yawned and looked around her,

instantly aware of the stiff sting in her neck. Wincing, she realized she had stayed too long in the sun. "Oh, Fletcher, my back. Is it bad?"

"Let's just say a male lobster would find you very attractive." He pushed damp wisps of hair away from her face, then frowned. "Why did you fall asleep, Casey? You know better than that."

"Don't scold. Just help me into the house—but don't touch me." She lifted herself slowly as the heat radiated through her body. "I don't know how I could've been so foolish. I just felt so tired."

Fletcher took her hand and led her to the patio door. Sliding the glass, he touched her shoulder to help her through when she stiffened and gasped.

"Don't touch me!"

"Sorry, I forgot."

She stood, arms held away from her body, in the living room and let the cool air circulate around her. Soothing as it was, the air couldn't dissipate the burning heat that was concentrated on her back and legs. Even the soles of her feet stung as Fletcher surveyed her in all her discomfort, her hand pressed against her throbbing forehead.

"Where are Mack and Ella?" she asked, expecting one of them to appear.

"I guess Ella's gone to town. It's her day off, and there's no telling where Mack is," Fletcher replied with a shrug. "Go upstairs and lie down while I get some evaporated milk to put on that burn."

Nodding, she forced herself slowly to the hall, every movement reminding her of the nagging pain she would feel for the rest of the day. Finally she reached her room and gingerly lay facedown, spread-eagled, on the bed.

Evaporated milk. The thought was nauseating, but she knew Fletcher wouldn't find any. For every sunburn she'd ever had, that was his suggested cure, but they never

54

seemed to have any in the house. So Fletcher had always come up with an equally disgusting substitute. She heard his determined footsteps.

"Well, we don't have any evaporated milk," he said apologetically. She smiled knowingly, bracing herself for the miracle cure.

"Well, Fletcher, what gross indignity am I to suffer this time?"

"This time it's buttermilk. I think it'll do the job. Slip into this little number, and I'll get to work," he said, tossing a bath towel to her side.

"You mean I have to get up again?" She sighed and reached for the terribly inadequate-looking towel.

"Not necessarily. I'd be glad to—"

"I'll get up." Stiffly Casey dragged herself to the bathroom and piled a black cloud of hair atop her head, then secured it with pins. Examining herself in the mirror, she noticed that both cheeks were equally roasted. She must have turned her head in her sleep. But a very conspicuous white line ran the length of her nose, flanked by two red splotches on each side.

Very cute, she told herself dryly, wrinkling her nose. The shooting pain made her relax it quickly. With utmost care Casey removed the tank suit and draped the towel loosely around her. When she opened the door again, Fletcher's casually interested gaze roaming over her made Casey clutch the terry cloth to her breasts. She swallowed self-consciously. "This must be the smallest towel in the house."

"I know. I thought I'd never find it." With a subtle wink, he cocked his head toward the bed. "Climb in. I'll try to be gentle."

She drew an involuntary breath and eyed him warily as she crawled onto the bed. "You always say that, Fletcher."

"Uh-huh," he drawled. "And I always am."

She shivered and gasped as the first drops of cold liquid oozed onto her tender skin. Waiting for his faint, yet excruciating touch, she stiffened. His fingers made a widening circle on her back, coaxing her to relax as he gently spread the soothing buttermilk.

"Casey, remember the time we were sailing in the Caribbean?"

Oh, yes. She could never forget her first experience with swimming in the nude—its benefits *and* drawbacks. "We didn't have evaporated milk then, either."

"True, but I think the cottage cheese took the sting out, don't you?"

"Yes, but the smell . . ." She heard his chuckle and imagined his blue eyes twinkling.

"It wasn't so bad," he whispered. "I thought you and the sliced peaches made a delectable dessert."

She knew the sudden light-headed tingling was not a side effect of the sunburn. It was the memory—a vivid picture—of Fletcher's magnificent nude body approaching her on a secluded Jamaican beach. She had watched in fascination the leonine movement of his compact hips and muscular thighs, the rise and fall of his bronzed, hair-covered chest. He seemed totally unconscious of his own overwhelming maleness. She had been held breathless by his unmistakable desire and his determination to have it fulfilled. Casey quickly blinked the vision away, but the scintillating circular motions of Fletcher's hands on her spine threatened to bring it back again. "I think that's enough, Fletcher," she announced.

"Right," he agreed. "We'll go to your legs now." His fingers shifted to the backs of her thighs, slowly rubbing, stroking, spreading the thick creamy liquid. "Then there was that time on the Riviera," he continued. "You couldn't wear clothes for two days."

"*I* had a sunburn, Fletcher. What was *your* excuse?"

"Ah, three years later you finally ask." He chuckled softly. "Would you believe I didn't want you to feel self-conscious?"

"No," she murmured, suppressing a smile. "But it *was* nice, wasn't it? The freedom, the fun . . ."

"The frustration."

She smothered her laughter into the pillow. "Didn't the cold showers help?"

"Not when I took them with you," he growled.

"Oh . . . yes." Showers with Fletcher. Tasting, exploring, reveling in the moist scent of him until her sunburn was nothing compared to the heated passion between them.

"We used vinegar that time, didn't we?" he asked as his fingers slid once or twice to the insides of her thighs.

"Pickle juice." It could've been a slip of his hands, she supposed, but if it happened again . . .

"What did you say?"

She gasped with indignation. "Pickle juice, Fletcher, and I'm not burned *there!*" Cool caution stirred within her. She turned onto her side to eye him suspiciously.

With upturned, milky palms he shrugged. "A totally innocent mistake, I assure you. I'm surprised you can think about sex at a time like this."

"I am *not* thinking about sex."

"Well, it's a good thing because, in your condition . . ." With a devilish squint he rubbed his chin with the back of his hand. "But you know, if you're determined, we could probably think of a way. . . . We've done it before."

She drew a deep breath, knowing the heat in her cheeks wasn't caused entirely by the sun. When she saw the seductive tilt of his smile, the deceptively innocent eyes, she was almost tempted . . . completely tempted. Casey sighed with exasperation. "Are you quite finished?"

"Yes. There doesn't seem to be much more I can do right now." He leaned over and playfully kissed her nose, then straightened and looked into her eyes.

"Why did you do that, Fletcher?" she asked softly.

"Oh, I don't know," he replied, wiping his fingers on a hand towel. "I never could resist that alluring scent. Curdled Conquest, isn't it?"

"Get serious." She reached for a pillow and flung it at him, but he tossed it aside.

"Okay," he said with mock severity. "You take a shower, then come downstairs to the kitchen. I'll be working on a very serious omelet."

She had to laugh at the stubborn set of his mouth. "With cheese, I hope. That's my favorite."

"I wouldn't have it any other way, Casey."

Something about his sincere tone and the benevolent look in his eyes before he left the room made her heart skip a beat. She was thankful he was gone and couldn't see the confusion in *her* eyes. Now he was the same old Fletcher, laughing, joking, lightly affectionate, but, at other times, she could only think how much he had changed. Of course, one day was hardly a basis for comparison.

She decided to give herself more time to form an opinion. Right now the only thing she knew for sure was that the charming Priscilla was definitely after her ex-husband, and that Fletcher was definitely not discouraging her. Somehow Casey couldn't see them together, unless Fletcher had changed a lot more than she realized.

That's really none of my business, Casey reminded herself, frowning. Fletcher had a right to live his life any way he saw fit, and if Priscilla was the one he wanted, well— No. No, she couldn't convince herself of indifference toward Fletcher. He was too much a part of her life for that. Neither could she dismiss the fact that he was still very attractive to her, but that was surely only temporary.

After all, Fletcher was a charming, desirable man. She'd been married to him for two years. No one could expect her to be completely unaffected by his good looks. Looks that had only improved with the years, she thought, irritated. But, with time, she could look at him as just another good friend.

"Liar, liar, pants on fire" danced through her mind as she walked mechanically to the shower and turned on the tap. As acutely as she felt the cracks in the dried milk on her flesh, Casey could see the cracks in her theory. Time would never make her see him as merely a good friend. Time would only make her love him or hate him. There could be no room for in-between.

CHAPTER FOUR

Surveying herself with a critical eye, Casey stepped closer
to the full-length mirror and turned for a side view of her
white crepe de chine evening dress.

What a waste of a beautiful, expensive outfit, she
thought with a frown. But the backless halter-top dress
was the only one she had brought that wouldn't irritate
her sunburn. It was her "just in case" dress. She had held
it in reserve "just in case" she was ever asked to the
Presidential Inaugural Ball or "just in case" some irresist-
ible man invited her to dance in the moonlight on the
rooftop of a swank hotel. And now she was wearing it for
a simple business dinner with Henry Ames and Priscilla.

She sighed. At least Fletcher would be there to admire
the soft fine lines of the dress that plunged shockingly to
her waist. She smiled, thinking of the appreciative look she
knew would be forthcoming in his blue-gray eyes when he
saw her floating down the stairs. She might not be as good
as Priscilla was at floating, but there was hope. Yes, Casey
thought, as she smoothed the natural arch of her dark
brows with a slender finger. As long as she was going to
wear the dress, she might as well go all the way.

She sat at her dressing table and applied smokey-gray eyeshadow to her lids, then beneath her long lower lashes. That was the look she wanted, she thought. Sultry, but not too flashy. Casey played with one of the wavy wisps of black hair that framed her face, then patted the loosely swirled topknot at the crown of her head.

The overall effect was stunning, she had to admit, but something was missing. She opened the black velvet jewel case on the table and took out two teardrop earrings, which shimmered with diamonds. After all, nothing else would do with this dress, she reminded herself. She fastened them into her pierced ears, then lifted from the box the matching braided platinum chain with its larger diamond teardrop. When it rested around her neck, Casey moved back to the full-length mirror to turn from side to side, watching the facets of the stones twinkle at her.

Hmmm. Fletcher might miss the dress and he might miss her hair, but he couldn't help but notice the diamonds at her throat and ears, she thought with a little smile, then a frown.

What was she doing? Trying to give Priscilla competition? Well, why not? Casey stared haughtily into the mirror and decided Priscilla was a little too sure of herself, anyway. A soft tap at the door ended Casey's reverie. She took one last look at her hair.

"Come in."

"Casey, they're here. Are you re—" Fletcher stopped short, wrapping his fingers around the doorknob as his gaze traveled boldly over her, sending tingles of vain pleasure up and down her spine. Her breath caught as it always had when Fletcher looked at her in that slow, caressing way. The survey taken, his brows lifted slightly, communicating approval. "Are you ready?"

"Of course. How do I look?" She twirled slowly, wanting to hear the compliment she read in his eyes.

"You look beautiful and you know it." He smiled with obvious admiration. "Is that a new dress?"

"Oh, no. I've had it for ages."

"I see. Just run-of-the-mill attire for boring business dinners," Fletcher said dryly. "I doubt if certain people will be thinking of oil wells tonight."

"What do you mean?" Casey straightened her shoulders. "I can discuss business, no matter what I'm wearing."

"I was referring to Henry and me."

"Oh, well, I can't help what Henry Ames thinks, and I certainly can't be held responsible for the wanderings of your mind." She smiled with pretended shyness.

"The way you look tonight, you will *definitely* be held responsible." The seductive promise in his tone kept her from making a flip retort. She could only stare into his eyes and listen to the pounding of her own heart. His regretful sigh preceded a low chuckle. "Will you come with me now, or would you rather make a grand entrance?"

"A queen never goes anywhere unescorted."

"Well, does a queen wear shoes?" His gaze rested on the hem of her dress, and Casey couldn't help curling her nylon-clad toes.

So much for regal behavior, she thought, wrinkling her nose as she walked to the closet door and slipped her feet into white satin sandals.

"Leave it to you, Fletcher, to find the flaw."

"I suppose it was rather common of me." He shrugged and feigned disappointment. "Does that mean I have to walk three steps behind you, Your Grace?"

"Since you wouldn't do it anyway, there's no point in insisting. But one more slip like that, and you shall be banished from the kingdom."

"Hmmm. Just like last time," he murmured.

62

"Come on, Fletcher," she said, taking his arm. "I was only joking."

"Sometimes your jokes come dangerously close to the truth." Fletcher led her from the bedroom to the landing, then turned her to him. "Only this time I won't be banished so easily." His lips softly brushed her cheek, and she felt a sharp intake of breath. It couldn't really be called a kiss, and yet the gentle touch of his lips set her pulse pounding the way it always had when she knew he was about to make love to her.

What did he mean by that? Was he planning to come back into her life? She felt as though her feet couldn't move until she knew the answer. She turned her gaze to him for some sign, but there was nothing in his eyes to tell her.

"Come on, Casey. Your audience awaits," he teased and nudged her down the steps.

Damn him! She had wanted to float downstairs, and now it was all she could do to pick her way to the bottom. He always dropped some remark like that, designed to titillate her, confuse her. Now she'd be lucky if she didn't tumble all the way to the first floor and land at Priscilla's feet. Well, two could play at that game. She would add a little confusion of her own to the evening.

When they reached the last step, she sighed nervously.

"Relax, Casey. You're not going into battle."

I wouldn't bet on that, a small voice reared inside her. But, if Fletcher was foolish enough to take a chance, then he should put his money on her, because she was determined to win. She flashed her most gracious smile and allowed him to lead her to the living room, where Mack was serving cocktails to Priscilla and, Casey presumed, Henry. Casey silently thanked the stars for her own white dress. The black one she had almost chosen would surely have made her look like Hard-hearted Hannah next to

63

Priscilla, who was dressed in a cloud of pink that emphasized her almost iridescent skin and fine blond hair. Priscilla immediately took command of Fletcher's other arm.

"Don't you look nice, darling. That suit matches your eyes perfectly," Priscilla said, brushing a lock of his hair into place. "But that hair. What are we going to do about that? We must find you a new stylist."

"Casey's the only one who could ever cut his hair to suit him," Mack gruffly interjected from the bar. "She looks great tonight, don't you think?"

"Why, yes, that dress really flatters your figure, Casey," Priscilla said with an innocent smile.

"Thanks, Priscilla." Casey released Fletcher's arm and walked to Mack's side. "My mother always said I clean up well." She felt Fletcher's stare bore into her flesh and silently chalked up one for her team.

Priscilla ignored the remark. "Casey, you haven't met Daddy yet. Daddy, stand up and meet Fletcher's *ex*-wife, Casey—Robbins, isn't it? You *did* keep Fletcher's last name, didn't you?"

Casey squared her shoulders and smiled. "How do you do, Mr. Ames." She held out a hand to a balding, heavyset man with sparsely lashed brown eyes—eyes that looked at his daughter as though he were fully prepared to step in front of an oncoming train rather than have Priscilla suffer one moment of indignity.

"Nice to meet you, Mrs. Robbins." The gaze he turned to Casey made her wonder if he would rather have her, Casey, in front of the oncoming train. He touched her fingers only slightly, then settled himself on the sofa while sipping his drink.

"Well, Casey, you and I are the only ones without a drink. What'll you have?" Fletcher asked, releasing himself from Priscilla's clutches. He stepped to the bar and looked at Casey questioningly.

"Why, whatever you're— Uh, I think I'd like a tequila sunrise."

"Sounds good. Maybe I'll have one myself." But Fletcher didn't begin mixing the drinks immediately. He only stared at her as though he remembered, as she did, a time when tequila sunrises had heralded his every glorious homecoming from long business trips.

She turned away, thinking of a time when each breathless return was a new beginning for her and Fletcher. A new sunrise that opened her heart like a spring flower, unfolding its petals as though Fletcher were the sun, drawing her to him.

He had driven the mist from her eyes with clever words like "What's the matter? Have Mack's stories finally reduced you to tears?"

And she had responded with equally urbane statements like "No, I'm just trying to remember who you are, that's all."

Then he had searched her body and mind for recognition, for reassurance of their love, and she had reveled in total abandon in his arms—still-full glasses of tequila sunrise sat sweating on the bedside table.

Now she felt a tear escape the prison of her eye to slip down her cheek and veil the memory.

God, what am I doing? she asked herself, wiping the intruder away. To think that a stupid drink could make her have such intense feelings in front of all these people! She bit her lower lip to stop its despicable quivering and turned back to Fletcher.

"On second thought, Fletcher, I'd—"

"It's done, Casey." He lifted her hand and pressed her fingers around the chilled glass. "Don't change your mind now." His mouth curved into a smile tinged with—with what? Sadness? Just as quickly as it had come the smile was gone, and he walked away from her to draw his other guests into conversation.

Casey lingered at the bar a moment while she sipped her drink and tried to regain her composure. The cool, fruity taste helped to soothe her raw emotions and slide her tilted perspective back into place.

Fletcher was right. It was done. Her marriage was over and, for better or worse, she had accepted it. So why the futile raking of the coals? *Buck up,* she told herself stubbornly. A chair. She needed her own easy chair. As Casey turned toward it Priscilla's wide blue eyes greeted hers against the background of china-blue upholstery.

Mentally shaking herself for the possessive feeling that stirred warmly through her, Casey drifted to Fletcher's side and perched on the arm of his chair. She almost laughed at Priscilla's instant reaction.

"Oh, I'm sorry," she said, half-rising. "I know this is your favorite chair. I wouldn't dream of taking it."

"Don't be silly, Priscilla. I'm just fine where I am." With a small feline smile Casey lazily draped her arm on the back of Fletcher's chair, brushing the hard muscles of his neck with an accidental caress. Feeling his skin shiver slightly beneath her touch, she instinctively patted his shoulder and tried to appear interested in the small talk he had started with Henry and Mack.

But Mack would have none of it, Casey thought. His gaze met hers and, together, they shared a silent chuckle. That old rascal hadn't missed a trick so far and, for the moment, Casey felt relieved that Mack's son was not quite so perceptive; for Mack saw her as she was and accepted her. Casey feared that Fletcher might not be so charitable.

"I'd like to propose a toast." Fletcher lifted his half-drained glass. "Here's to our newly formed oil company and to the geologist who's going to tell us where the crude is hiding."

With the sound of tinkling crystal Casey smiled a "thank you" as Mack and Henry joined the salute.

"I'd like to get in on this, too." Priscilla came forward with a pouting expression and rested on the other arm of Fletcher's chair. "I *am* a partner, you know."

"Of course, Priscilla." Fletcher lifted his glass in confirmation, then finished his drink.

Casey smiled inwardly, wondering if Fletcher were enjoying himself or if he felt somewhat like a prisoner, flanked by armed guards in his own home. The amused look in Mack's eyes told her that her ex-father-in-law was thinking along the same mischievous lines.

"Well, isn't this cozy?" Priscilla sighed and looked toward her father, then Mack. "You're unusually quiet tonight, Mack. Any special reason?"

"No. Just thinking." Mack kept his eyes straight ahead as he puffed on a thick cigar.

"Oh, about what?" Priscilla asked in a conciliatory tone. "I'd love to know what's put that mysterious twinkle in your eye."

Glancing quickly from Mack to Priscilla, Casey wondered if the wide-eyed blonde had finally pushed Mack too far.

No, he wouldn't dare! Casey thought with rising discomfort. She felt Fletcher stiffen beside her and struggled to think of a way to keep Mack quiet.

"Mostly I was thinking about wishbones," Mack stated philosophically.

Priscilla stared in confusion. "What do wishbones have to do with anything?"

Don't ask, Casey silently begged as she lowered her gaze to the floor and waited for the answer.

Mack continued tapping his cigar on the edge of an ashtray. "Well, I was just thinking that if each of you ladies grabbed one of Fletcher's legs . . ."

Casey jumped from her seat in alarm. "Fletcher, I'm sure dinner is ready by now."

"Good. I'm starved. Let's go, Priscilla." Fletcher took Priscilla's hand and quickly led her toward the dining room as Henry followed.

Casey lingered behind to wrap her fingers tightly around Mack's arm. "Mack, what are you trying to do?" she whispered. "I've never seen Fletcher run out of a room like that."

"Don't worry about Fletcher. I can handle him. I just don't like the way that *jezebel* is treating you."

"Oh, Mack." She smoothed his beard affectionately. "I know you did that for me but, honestly, don't you think you're being too hard on Priscilla? She's really not so bad, you know."

"I suppose so," he admitted, snuffing his cigar. "But seeing her in *your* chair, trying to take *your* place, well . . ."

She smiled at the blue eyes that were so like Fletcher's. His fierce loyalty, his devotion swelled her throat with love until she could hardly speak. But she must. "Things can never be like they were, Mack. And I'm afraid antagonizing Priscilla won't help the situation."

"But, damn it, Casey, you could—"

"No . . . no, I couldn't," she said with a gentle shake of her head. "Now, let's join the others and try to behave ourselves for the rest of the evening." She held out a hand. "Deal?"

"A deal," he grumbled, sealing the bargain with a halting handshake. Linking her arm with his, Casey couldn't suppress a smile at this and other times she had struck similar bargains with Mack.

Upon entering the dining room Casey immediately noticed Fletcher's preferred seating arrangement. Resentment flared, but she choked it back, knowing her feelings were unjustified. Fletcher presided at one end of the burnished oak table with Priscilla seated as hostess at the opposite end, while Henry had taken a place between them. Casey decided to view the situation with a measure of grace as Mack held the chair beside Henry for her, then seated himself on the opposite side.

After all, I'm not mistress at the Circle R anymore, Casey reminded herself. She had no rights as hostess. Still, it hurt to think that Priscilla had taken her place in more ways than one.

While Ella served the soup and Priscilla led the conversation, Casey's eyes focused on the huge mural that covered the opposite wall. She never tired of examining its many scenes of life in Texas, from the coast of Corpus Christi on up to the bright lights of Dallas to the north. Her gaze kept returning to her favorite scene of the Santa Gertrudis bull that grazed in a rolling grassland, symbolizing the Circle R.

Casey smiled, supposing that some people might think it in bad taste to have a picture of a bull in the dining room amidst all the antique furniture and Spanish candelabra, but she couldn't share that opinion. The sturdy Santa Gertrudis had been the basis for the perpetual wealth and prosperity on the ranch. Although a local interior decorator had once suggested a less imposing mural to complement the elegant decor of the room, Fletcher and Mack—well, Fletcher, anyway—had graciously declined.

"Ella, you're slipping." Casey heard Mack's gruff voice. "This soup is cold."

"It's vichyssoise. It's supposed to be cold," Casey whispered, signaling Mack with a warning frown, but he only stared at his bowl of soup.

"Yes, Miss Ames suggested it for tonight," Ella stated before promptly leaving the room.

"Priscilla, you *asked* for cold potato soup?" Mack

shook his head in disbelief. "Why, I never heard of such a"—he caught Fletcher's icy glare—"such an unusual idea." Mack lifted a spoonful to his mouth, pursing his lips as though the soup were of hemlock. "Hmmm. It's real tasty, Priscilla. I really like it."

Casey knew Mack would be ever so grateful if Ella would only serve the next course as soon as possible.

Mercifully Ella did serve delicious chicken in a red wine sauce, and Casey savored its tangy taste along with the braised carrots and creamed cauliflower. A light angel food cake, topped with chilled cling peaches, rounded out the meal, and when Ella returned to clear the table, Casey laid her napkin aside and smiled.

"Ella, you haven't lost your touch. The dinner was wonderful."

"Thank you, Mrs. Robbins. I always enjoy cooking for someone who appreciates good food," Ella said with an amused sideways glance at Mack.

"How long do you intend to stay here, Mrs. Robbins?" Henry's question sounded innocent enough, but Casey detected a hostile undercurrent in his tone.

"Please, call me Casey." She bestowed her most courteous smile. "I promised Fletcher I'd stay until you bring in the first well."

"I hardly think that's necessary," Henry said, raising his eyebrows. "If you'll just read the seismology graphs and tell us where to drill, I'm sure we can take care of the rest."

"Henry, I've asked Casey to do a little more than just read graphs." Fletcher's tone was full of patience, but Casey knew by the stubborn set of his cleft chin that Fletcher had braced himself for a disagreement, so she settled herself to watch him in action.

"What other duties did you have in mind for Casey?"

Priscilla asked with a wide-eyed innocence that set Casey's teeth on edge.

"She'll act as liaison between me and the seismology team," Fletcher explained. "As you know, they'll be blasting, and I don't want the cattle disturbed. Casey and I will work together and come up with a schedule for moving the cattle to coincide with the blasting. Then, of course, when the drilling begins, she'll be my agent. I am, after all, a cattleman."

It was all matter-of-fact and to the point, but Casey noted with annoyance that Henry remained unconvinced.

"It seems an unnecessary expense to me," Henry said in clipped tones.

"Since I've agreed to shoulder this particular expense, I'll decide whether or not it's necessary." Although patience was still evident in his voice, Fletcher's eyes flashed a steely gray.

Not like the Fletcher she once knew, Casey thought in confusion. Fletcher rarely allowed himself the luxury of anger, but he was clearly on the verge of it now.

"Well, I can't wait for our first gusher," Priscilla said with a smile that didn't quite reach her eyes.

"I'm afraid you're in for a disappointment." Fletcher turned a softer gaze to Priscilla. "Gushers are a waste of good crude. Only an irresponsible accident would cause one these days with modern technology. I thought you'd know that, considering that Henry's in the business of drilling wells."

Priscilla shrugged in defense. "Daddy and I never discuss business much."

"Give her time, Fletcher." Henry smiled at his daughter. "Priscilla is new at this, and I'm not so sure that a woman should bother herself too much with this sort of thing."

"Oh, really?" Casey could keep quiet no longer at

71

Henry's cavalier attitude. "Not even when she has so much invested? Why, if it was my money—"

"There's no need to upset yourself, Casey, since it isn't *your* money," Henry said condescendingly. "I realize that some women have to make their own way in the world when they don't have husbands to do it for them. I don't mind that as long as they're not too pushy." He patted Casey's head sympathetically, and she felt her anger seethe beneath his touch. "But in Priscilla's position—"

"Mr. Ames, I am not a Saint Bernard. *Please,* don't treat me like one." Casey struggled to control the erratic rise and fall of her breasts. She marveled at Henry's unabashed chuckle as his hand returned to the table and he continued his infuriating commentary.

"As I was saying, in Priscilla's position she needs someone to guide her in business matters."

"Oh, I see. A benevolent despot." Casey shook her head in cynicism.

"If you will." Henry shrugged.

"Well, I won't!" Casey snapped. "Henry Ames, you have to be the most—"

"Casey! That's enough." The sound of Fletcher's cold voice brought her gaze up to meet his matching stare. "Could I see you in the study for a moment?" He turned to Priscilla. "Would you ask Ella to bring coffee to the living room? We'll join you there shortly."

With her most dignified posture Casey strolled to the double doors of the study and opened them. Walking to Fletcher's desk, she saw the contract she had signed that morning. Resisting the urge to rip it to pieces, Casey turned away and moved to the window. She felt calmer now, although the sting of Fletcher's words still cut through her thoughts and left them strewn about her mind.

The click of the closing door brought her around to face

Fletcher. Biting back stinging words of her own, Casey watched him come toward her. Alarm rippled through her at the forbidding slant of his brows. His dark eyes were cold and steady. Even with their menacing threat her body quivered with tingling appreciation. For one irrational moment she wanted to walk into his embrace and let the roughness of his kiss soothe her wounded pride. But the rigid set of his broad shoulders warned her to stay where she was. Casey recognized his nearness as a blatant attempt to make her feel small, but she couldn't back away.

"Casey, you and Mack have done everything in your power to sabotage this evening."

"Sabotage?" She lifted her chin a little higher. "What did you want me to do, Fletcher? Lick Henry's hand? Maybe lie at his feet while he bestowed more pearls of wisdom on us?"

"Of course not. He didn't mean anything by what he did. He does that to Priscilla all the time, and I don't see her getting so upset."

"I'm *not* Priscilla."

"So I've noticed." His features, taut with the effort of controlling his anger, seemed to relax a bit. Fletcher stepped even closer as his warm breath fanned her forehead. His hands moved to her shoulders in a smooth caress that both annoyed and aroused her. "Now, listen to me. As of this morning, you work for me *and* Henry *and* Priscilla. I'm paying you a good salary. At the very least you could be a little more gracious."

"No, *you* listen to me, Fletcher." Every muscle strained to deny the delicious feel of his skin against hers. "I don't need this aggravation. You know what you can do with your money. I'm not staying." Casey turned away, stubbornly folding her arms across her breasts.

"Casey, you signed a contract."

"Contracts can be dissolved."

73

He grabbed her arm and spun her around to face him. "Only when both parties are willing. I'm not."

"So sue me," she countered, cocking an eyebrow.

"You may depend on that if you don't live up to the bargain."

"You wouldn't dare."

"Try me." His voice was cool, as if he knew he had won. And she knew it, too. He let out a sigh and shook his head. "Now, let's go back in there and enjoy ourselves. Any thinking woman would know how to handle a man like Henry. I'm sure you could've found a more tactful way to set him straight."

"I've always thought the straightforward approach was best."

"Take it from me. It doesn't always get you what you want." The tiny lines that fanned out from his eyes seemed a little deeper tonight. Casey suddenly wanted to stroke them, to soothe them away. Instead, she sighed wearily, feeling the strain of the evening.

"Okay, maybe I did get upset over nothing. After all, I've met men with Henry's attitude more than once. Perhaps I just never thought I'd meet one here. That's all."

With a patient smile he pulled her to him and kissed the tip of her nose. "You won't be seeing that much of Henry. Most of the time you'll be working with me."

He stood staring intently at her lips. His finger slowly and deliberately traced the outline of her full mouth. Then bringing his lips to meet hers, he brushed them provocatively, enticingly. Beneath his searching gaze her stubbornness melted to begrudging resignation. Casey was fully aware that she was once again being manipulated, but the tenderness of his touch was too alluring, his coaxing half-smile too breathtaking. She was robbed of the strength to argue. For now, anyway.

When she entered the living room, Casey sat beside

74

Mack on the sofa. Her reassuring wink erased the concerned look on the bearded man's face.

"Where's Henry?" Fletcher asked no one in particular.

"Daddy asked me to convey his regrets. He had a late business meeting that he couldn't get out of." Priscilla walked to Fletcher and straightened his tie.

"I hope he didn't leave on my account," Casey said. A faint feeling of guilt and the conviction that she was right waged a battle in her mind.

"Oh, no, Casey." Priscilla sank onto the easy chair and motioned Fletcher to sit on the arm. "Daddy understands that we women can be ... well, quite emotional at times."

Conviction suddenly found its second wind. Casey shook her head with disgust. "Priscilla, you and your father—must accept my apology," she said when her gaze collided with Fletcher's raised brows.

"Of course." Priscilla smiled. "I guess it's been difficult for you, Casey. Coming back here after being away for so long, finding everything so ... different. I met up with an old friend of yours the other day," she went on in a considerably brighter tone, "someone who seemed very pleased to hear you'd be in town for a while. You remember Steve Howard, I'm sure? He was wondering whether he should call you or not, and naturally, I said—"

"Absolutely not," Fletcher cut in. He rose and walked to the bar, then began tossing ice cubes into a glass. "For the time being, Casey will be much too busy for that. Priscilla, I think you should let Casey take care of her own social life."

"Why, Fletcher!" Priscilla joined him at the bar. "You act as though I've just asked her to go out with Atilla the Hun. I thought you liked Steve."

"There's nothing wrong with Steve Howard," Fletcher stated flatly.

"Now that he's met with your approval," Casey flared,

"I'd *like* to see Steve." The nerve of those two! Fletcher and Priscilla were talking as though she, Casey, weren't even in the room, as though she were a child and they were deciding what boarding school she should attend. Well, she had no burning desire to go out with Steve, but she damned sure wasn't going to let her ex-husband make the decision for her. "Yes, I'd love to see Steve again."

"No, no." Priscilla shook her head. "If Fletcher disapproves, then I shouldn't have said a word. I'll tell Steve you're not available when I see him again."

"You'll tell him no such thing." Casey lifted her chin and matched Fletcher's cold stare. "Now that I know Steve's interested, I can take it from here, Priscilla. You won't have to risk Fletcher's disapproval again."

"Come on, Priscilla. I'll take you home if you're ready." Fletcher set his drink on the bar and reached for Priscilla's arm.

"You know, darling," Priscilla said as she walked with Fletcher toward the hall. "This all reminds me of that Shakespeare sonnet you read to me."

"Shakespeare?" Casey asked, frowning. "Fletcher quotes Shakespeare?"

Priscilla turned to face her. "Why, yes. Didn't he ever? . . ." She smiled shyly. "Well, I guess he has to be in the mood."

"I'll leave you and Mack to entertain each other for a while," Fletcher said flippantly. "Try not to plot the overthrow of the U.S. government while I'm gone. You two are in such rare form tonight that you might succeed."

"Oh, I don't know," Mack said, stretching lazily. "I was thinking of a rousing game of pool. How about you, Casey?"

"Sounds good to me." Casey shrugged indifferently, realizing that of all the feelings inside her, indifference was definitely not one of them. She had set herself up for a date with a man she had no wish to see and made Fletcher angry again in the bargain. Her thoughts were more confused than ever. Why was Fletcher so against her seeing Steve when their marriage was over? It must be his ego. That was the only answer that came to mind. Well, she had one of those too, and after the beating it had taken tonight, hers deserved a little boost, even if it came in the form of Steve Howard.

When Fletcher and Priscilla had left, Casey lost one game of pool to Mack, then begged off the second. Pleading a headache, she excused herself and went upstairs to her room, where she kicked off her shoes and stretched out on the bed.

Wiggling her toes, she allowed the events of the evening to flood her mind, hoping that some sense of perspective would spring up and make things clear again, but no revelations appeared, and she rose to wander restlessly into the sitting room. She noticed Fletcher's chess set on the game table near the wall. Each piece was in its proper place, as if waiting to do battle with the aid of two worthy opponents.

Casey picked up the onyx king and absently stroked its smooth edges.

How this king would jeer if she should attempt a game of chess in her present state of mind. *I should be content,* Casey thought with a sigh. After all, she had a new assignment and, at any other time, her work would have loomed foremost in her thoughts. But it wasn't enough anymore. She should stop hiding—yes, hiding—she told herself when her thoughts turned toward excuses at the word. Stop hiding behind core samples and seismology graphs. There was more to life than her career.

But what? Love? Marriage? She had tried both and failed miserably. Anyway, she didn't know if she even liked Fletcher anymore. He preferred the clinging kind now. And to think that he had always made such cutting remarks about women like that while they were married. The memory made her angry all over again. She could have met him halfway had she known he would change so drastically. Casey frowned at the black king that lay in the palm of her hand. Shakespeare, indeed.

"How about a friendly match for old time's sake?"

Casey looked up to see Fletcher, barefoot as he stood at his bedroom door. He seemed totally engrossed in the act of rolling up his shirt-sleeves. As she watched each tanned forearm appear from beneath the silky fabric, Casey became more interested herself. Too interested for her own good, she admitted flatly.

Fletcher had removed his tie and loosened his collar. Casey groaned inwardly at the thatch of feathery hair peeking out from his shirt, unbuttoned below the middle of his broad chest. Her eyes moved down to the trim, belted waist and lean hips. His blue slacks concealed the muscles of his thighs, but it didn't matter. Every inch of Fletcher's body was etched clearly in her memory so that she would never forget. God, he was a big man, and not an ounce of excess fat anywhere.

"Well, how about it?" he asked, his question jerking her gaze from the middle of his thigh.

Ignoring the amusement that settled in one corner of his mouth, she returned the chess piece to its domain and sighed. "No, thanks, I'm not in the mood for any more battles tonight."

"That's encouraging," he said with raised brows. "But what can we do to give this evening the decent burial it deserves?"

"Oh, I don't know. Why don't you quote some Shakespeare? That should do it."

"Why, I'd be happy to," he said, matching her soft sarcasm. He squared his shoulders in a patriotic pose, then cleared his throat. " 'Friends, Romans, countrymen . . .' "

"That's not quite what I had in mind, Fletcher."

His eyes widened slightly as he came toward her. "What exactly *did* you have in mind? Something a little more romantic, maybe?" Before she could retreat, he took her arm and nudged her toward the sofa. His hands rested on her shoulders for a moment before squeezing tenderly. "We need just the right atmosphere for this," he said, gently pushing her to the seat.

"Fletcher, I don't think—"

"Ah-ah," he admonished playfully. "I'm the director. Your head goes here." He patted a throw pillow at the end of the sofa. Eyeing him suspiciously, she obeyed but wondered if Fletcher weren't just a little too enthusiastic with his direction. When he scooped her feet from the floor and placed them in a horizontal position, she stiffened. But he paid absolutely no attention to her warning frown as he adjusted the hem of her dress. "Just give me the signal when you're ready," he said.

Then he stood above her, his arms crisscrossing his chest, waiting. She couldn't help but be affected by the sheer masculinity of him. The muscular arms, the flat stomach, the patient fingers that tapped against one elbow. Confidence seemed to emanate from *him* when *she* had none at all. Casey squirmed inside at the hint of amusement in his eyes.

" 'One if by land, and two if by sea,' " he prompted.

"That's Longfellow, not Shakespeare," she reminded him dryly, then shifted onto her side to support herself on one elbow.

He shook his head in mock dejection. "I always get those two confused."

"Sure. I think you're just reluctant to waste a sonnet on an ex-wife," she challenged.

There was no verbal response at first. But when his gaze slowly traveled the length of her, sounding an alarm in every nerve, her bravado shrank to tingling wonder. She saw desire push amusement aside in his eyes as he sat beside her and gently cupped her chin. The warmth of his touch set her pulse racing.

"Sonnets? You want sonnets?" he asked quietly.

She didn't speak. She *couldn't* speak. Only her eyes willed him to begin.

" 'Shall I compare thee to a summer's day? Thou art more lovely and more temperate . . .' "

Her skepticism faded with the deep, mellow tones of the words that he spoke. Mesmerized, she watched his supple lips form each syllable with velvet sounds that touched her soul. Her own mouth quivered in fascination, for she had read the familiar lines before but had never heard them imparted with such quiet, simple sincerity.

" '. . . But thy eternal summer shall not fade, Nor lose possession of that fair thou owest . . .' "

Even as the tip of his finger softly stroked her cheek, the exquisite tenderness in his voice stroked her heart, inviting her, daring her, compelling her to believe that the words were his own.

" '. . . So long as men can breathe, or eyes can see, So long lives this, and this gives life to thee.' "

Suddenly she *did* feel alive as her emerald eyes met the dawn of his gray ones. She parted her lips in silent consent, and his mouth covered hers in intimate understanding. His kiss was warm and searching, as though he craved her lips in the same way she hungrily desired his. When he released her, she felt a momentary pang of disappointment, then the delight of sweet reunion as he lowered himself beside her and took her in his arms. Molding her body to his, he kissed her again as he slipped the pins from her hair and ran gentle fingers through her raven tresses.

"God, your hair is lovely," he whispered, and she couldn't resist a dreamy smile when he snuggled in the soft curve of her shoulder.

She reveled in the delicious feel of his flesh against her throat. His feather kisses on her neck sent tiny shivers of desire echoing through her. She let out a soft moan and pulled him closer as he nibbled on the fleshy part of her ear. Her slender fingers entwined the thickness of his hair. When his lips found hers again his tongue glided inside her mouth to search the warmth of her yearning. She longed to feel his strong hands on her again. As if sensing her wish, his hand slipped up to untie the halter top at her neck. He lowered the dress to her waist, and she felt her nipples harden beneath his appreciative stare. She gasped at the touch of his teasing fingers.

Her gaze never left his fiery eyes as she unbuttoned his shirt and surrendered to the compulsive need to press her straining breasts against his hard chest. A soft groan escaped from deep within him. Caution sprang up to remind her of reality, to warn her not to give in to the hot swirls of passion that radiated through her being.

His hands reached out to frame her face with such tenderness that she couldn't look away. "Have you forgotten how good it was for us?" he asked, his voice thick with desire.

Shifting her hips slightly in protest, she gasped when his caressing palm molded her curves and thrust her against his hard body. Draping his lean, muscular thigh over her soft one, he locked her into his web of flaming intrigue from which she had neither will nor desire to escape. The need to be touched—to be touched by *him*—was overwhelming. Slowly, gently, constantly, he rocked her soul with magic caresses. His warm, moist kisses scattered her uncertain thoughts to oblivion, only to draw them together again as a single-minded slave to his will.

She cooperated fully when he slid the dress down past her hips to her feet, then dropped it carelessly onto the carpet. Then he turned his attention to her stockings, letting his hands glide over her legs, stopping to squeeze, caress.

"Very sexy," he said with an appreciative nod, "but they've gotta go." His gaze returned to capture hers with a seductive smile.

Oh, God, his smile was just as lethal, just as melting as ever. She welcomed the strong hand that slipped inside the waist of her stockings to palm her stomach. A shiver trailed the long, teasing stroke of his finger. Then both of his hands were inside, coaxing the nylon to her hips. She lifted slightly and heard his sharp intake of breath. She was filled with delight that tiny movements—her movements—like that could still excite him.

When her stockings had joined her dress, Fletcher's hands began a slow, thrilling reacquaintance with her body, taking in every curve, every recess. He laced his wanderings with hungry, probing kisses that left her weak and trembling.

"Undress me, Casey. Let me remind you how it used to be between us," he urged in a hoarse whisper.

His words sent waves of exciting anticipation thundering through her. Her heart pounded in the sheer confusion of it all. He wasn't her husband anymore. And yet she still wanted him every bit as much as she ever had. She reached for his belt buckle, her fingers quivering with the need to see all of him, to feel all of him. With his help she removed the barriers to her goal. His slacks, his underwear, the silky shirt, all came away under her impatient direction. Then she was back in his arms again. Silently he took her hand and placed it on him so that his need was unmistakable to her. As she caressed him, he fanned the flames of desire in her with a tantalizing search.

When he stood and crushed her to him, she sank against the warm hardness of him, engulfed in his embrace. His kiss was long and moist, leaving her mouth ravished as his hands entangled the ebony hair cascading over her creamy shoulders. He bent to kiss a waiting breast, covering the taut nipple with adoring, teasing lips. His tongue skimmed the rosy bud with agonizing thrusts. She clung to him, her eyes pleading total possession, her hands forcing his hips into her.

He held her away and swept her feet from the floor. As he carried her toward the bedroom she looked into his burning eyes and saw him smile.

"Now tell me you still want to go out with other men. Tell me anyone could make you feel better than this."

For a moment Casey could only stare at him and wonder if her ears had deceived her. But she knew they hadn't. She felt the color drain from her cheeks, then flood back in hot, crimson anger.

"Put me down!"

With a confused stare he complied and she turned away.

God, had he been thinking of her and Steve all the time he was— She closed her eyes and cringed at the humiliating thought. When she felt his hand gently caressing her shoulder, she pushed it away and turned on him with an icy glare.

"What the hell is wrong with you?" he asked with his hands on his narrow hips.

"Don't ever touch me again, Fletcher." Her breasts rose and fell steadily as she struggled to control the pain within her. "Why did you do it? To see if you could make me want you as much as I used to? Well, now you know."

"Casey, I—"

"Don't." She shrank from his outstretched fingers. "I

never thought you'd stoop to anything so shabby just to satisfy your ego."

"To hell with my ego!" he shouted. "Do you think I could—"

"Yes, you could. You *did!*" Her hand flew to her mouth and she turned away as she forced back tears.

"Casey, if I hurt you, I'm sorry," he whispered. Through closed eyes, hot tears spilled onto her cheeks and she heard his muffled footsteps on the carpet. "Oh, hell! Forget it."

She winced at the slam of his bedroom door.

CHAPTER FIVE

As soon as the seat belt sign faded Casey relaxed in her seat and sighed. At last she had time to catch her breath, she thought, smoothing the skirt of her beige jersey dress. She had hurried so to catch the early morning flight from Dallas to Victoria that she wondered if her luggage would be lost in the shuffle. Oh, well, it would catch up with her sooner or later, Casey decided, noting the empty seat beside her. If Fletcher were here, he would make sure— *Oh, don't do that,* she chided herself. *Don't think of him again. Fletcher isn't here.*

It was funny how she had been so eager to get away from him and now, after only two days, she was already missing his disagreeable blue-gray eyes and smugly confident manner. No, it wasn't funny, Casey corrected herself with a frown. It was pathetic. She could still hear the slam of his bedroom door, effectively ending all communication between them. She had left for Dallas the next afternoon without seeing him. Mack was the only one who seemed to care that she wanted to pick up some clothes at her apartment and check in at the office, then visit her sister before starting the work at the ranch. Fletcher hadn't even bothered to say good-bye, and Casey hadn't bothered to seek him out. She knew he was in the house that day, though. Each time he slammed another door, and he did that quite often, she *felt* his cool good-bye, as though he were pushing her further away; as though she had so hurt his pride that he couldn't stand the sight of her.

Well, he didn't have a monopoly on pride. How could he have been so insensitive? To think that she had been on the verge of— She felt her face grow hot at the thought. That was the way it had always been, though. She could be angry with him one moment, then on her way to his bed the next. She'd been a fool to think it could be otherwise.

Forcing thoughts of Fletcher from her mind, Casey pressed her nose against the window and watched with relief as the outskirts of Dallas faded from view. For the first time since moving there two years before, she felt curiously glad to be leaving the bustling throngs of people and never-ending traffic jams. Once she had thrived on the excitement and adventurous spirit of the city. Now she saw Dallas as just a network of twisting roads that seemed to lead nowhere, a mass of people, all speeding in different directions and stopping for no one.

Not really a fair assessment, Casey admitted grudgingly. She was just in one of her moods and knew that as soon as she stepped off the plane and saw her sister and three nephews, she would exchange her gloomy thoughts for more cheerful ones. Susan would be her punctual, serene self, as usual, although Casey didn't know how her sister managed it with three rowdy sons always clamoring for attention. Casey smiled, hoping the toy cars in her purse would keep the tough little guys quiet on the twenty-five-mile drive to their home in Port Lavaca. The boys would probably want "Aunt Casey" to take them fishing the way she always had on other visits. She would field their blunt, yet innocent questions about "Uncle Fletcher." How is he? Where is he? Why didn't he come, too? As if they had never even heard of divorce, she thought wryly.

Casey knew Fletcher had nurtured his relationship with her nephews, even after the divorce, and often wondered how he viewed the connection. Were they the children he'd never had? Or did he merely enjoy his lofty position as the favorite uncle who showered the boys with outrageous gifts and frequent, entertaining visits? Casey could find no answers. She had hardly hinted at her aching desire to have children, and Fletcher had never given any clue of his feelings on the subject. It was always her career he encouraged her to nurture and plan for, as if the possibility of children simply didn't exist. Then, when he had accused her of having an affair with Steve Howard, the question of children became a moot point.

Now, all that mattered was how she would deal with Fletcher during the time she worked for him. There was really only one answer, Casey supposed. She would have to keep her distance; not let him know how easily he could make her want him. Yes, that was the trick. She could do that, now that she knew *why* he wanted her.

Satisfied that she had the problem solved, Casey accepted a Coke from the flight attendant, then opened the novel on her lap to the first page. *Beware the Desert Prince,* the title read. *Make that prince a blond, and you've got yourself a deal,* Casey thought wryly, tossing her raven hair as she stroked the ivory ankh at her throat. With a sigh she turned her concentration to the book and its contents.

Some thirty minutes later Casey looked up in surprise when the voice of the attendant announced the end of the flight. Marking her place in the book, she gathered her belongings and followed the other passengers from the plane into the terminal. She couldn't resist a smile at the sight of the three small boys, bobbing up and down as though they were riding Pogo sticks. Just behind them stood Susan, her light brown hair swept away from her face and gathered with a polka-dot scarf at the nape of her neck.

Casey hardly had time to kiss the screwed-up faces of the tow-headed boys and hug her sister before Susan took charge and ushered them all to the baggage claim area, then out to the travel-worn station wagon.

The Rock of Gibraltar. That was the only way to describe Susan, Casey mused as she distributed the toy cars. But today there were lines of strain around Susan's blue eyes, and Casey wondered what could be the cause. She thought once about asking but sensed Susan's reticence and decided to wait until they could talk privately. Contenting herself with pleasant conversation, whenever the noise from the backseat permitted, Casey relaxed and enjoyed the scenic, sunny drive to Port Lavaca, a sleepy little town up the coast from Corpus Christi.

When they arrived at Susan's modest home, and the children were down for a nap, Casey took charge. Leading Susan to the kitchen, Casey pushed her sister onto a chair, then poured two cups of coffee.

"Susan, why don't you tell me what's wrong? If I didn't know better, I'd think you and John were expecting again," Casey said, raising her cup to her lips. When Susan didn't laugh at the joke, Casey set her coffee down again and shook her head. "Oh, no. Susan, how could you let that happen? Aren't three—"

"I'm not like you, Casey," Susan interrupted, bristling. "John and I are happy about it. Just because you never wanted any—"

"Now, what's that supposed to mean?"

"Nothing. Except that I know Fletcher always wanted children." Susan's voice was quiet as she lowered her gaze.

"Well, that's more than *I* know. He never said so to

me." Casey lifted her chin and refused to let the hurt and surprise she felt consume her.

"It always seemed to me that you two never talked openly about a lot of things. But all you have to do is watch him with my kids, and you'd know," Susan stated flatly.

"All right." Casey lifted her palms in concession, eager to shift the conversation away from the subject of Fletcher. "If the prospect of another child isn't the problem, then what's bothering you? Maybe I can help."

"It's John. He's not happy with his job." Susan's eyes began to mist before the words were out. "The company wants to transfer him. He'd rather stay here and go into business for himself."

"What's stopping him?" Casey asked, then closed her eyes and sighed as the answer dawned on her. "The new baby. You're feeling guilty about being pregnant and your understanding sister comes to pile on more guilt. I'm sorry." Casey reached across the table and patted her sister's hand.

"It's not only that." Susan rose and set her cup on the sink. "John's having trouble finding investors. You see, he wants to buy a fishing boat. There's a lot of money to be made when tourists come to Port Lavaca for deep sea fishing."

"Yes, I can imagine." Casey remembered how much she and Fletcher had paid for just one day's fishing off the coast of Corpus, and that was several years ago. "You know, that wouldn't be a bad investment for me."

"Oh, come on, Casey. Where would you get that kind of money?" Susan asked, sinking onto her chair with a sigh. "Geologists don't make *that* much."

"No, but I do own some land I could sell." Casey had no wish to sell any of her land, but if it would take that look of despair off her sister's face, well, a few acres, more or less, wouldn't make that much difference.

"I couldn't let you do that." Susan frowned, but Casey noticed a glimmer of hope in her sister's eyes.

"You know, the more I think about it, the better I like the idea. Don't say anything to John yet, though," Casey warned. "Tomorrow I'll talk to Fletcher and see if he's interested in buying back some of his land."

"Oh, you don't know what this will mean to us." Tears flowed freely from Susan's eyes, and Casey reached for a tissue from the kitchen counter. "We've been under such a strain lately. I guess it's brought us closer, though." Susan wiped the tears away and rose. "Perhaps, if you and Fletcher had struggled the way—"

"Uh, Susan." Casey hid her irritation with a forced smile of amusement. "I've just agreed to invest in your boat. Don't repay me with useless conjecture about what might have been."

"I should've known you'd feel that way." Susan hugged Casey and smiled. "You never look back, do you, Casey? A pillar of strength. That's you."

"Yes, just call me the Rock," Casey said dryly, returning Susan's embrace. Then she excused herself for a walk before the Rock crumbled into a million pieces under Susan's gaze of admiration.

Casey leaned back, resting her head on the grassy bank that sloped down to meet the clear, inviting water of the pond. With her jeans rolled up to her knees, she dangled her feet in the cool water, letting the tiny eddies swirl around her toes. Only the call of a single bobwhite claimed her attention as her gaze searched the surrounding trees for the source. Morning sunlight drifted through twisted branches to dapple the rippling water with shade, leaving Casey weak with drowsiness.

Her nephews were gone and all was quiet, she thought, gathering her shirttail into a knot just below her breasts. She smiled, thinking of her eager little fishing partners. In her mind she could still hear them arguing about who would carry the full stringer of perch to the house and who would clean them once they got there.

Casey reached for the frayed straw hat beside her and placed it on her head. Closing her eyes to the cool darkness, she felt for the baited cane pole nearby, then wrapped her fingers around it, lest another unsuspecting fish should bite while she rested.

Susan and John were lucky to have such a lush, peaceful corner of the earth, Casey mused with a sigh. No wonder they didn't want to give it up. Thoughts of her own property drifted through her mind, and Casey suppressed her twinge of irritation with Susan. Completely disregarding her wishes, Susan had blithely told John all about her offer to invest in the fishing boat the moment he set foot in the house the night before. Although cautioning John not to get his hopes up, Susan set about raising his expectations so high that Casey dreaded the possibility of Fletcher refusing her offer.

Remembering her own behavior, Casey rolled her eyes with regret in the darkness beneath the straw hat. Instead of tempering John's enthusiasm with a little common sense, she had allowed herself to get caught up in his contagious, go-getter attitude.

Now, as she lay in the shade of a twisted hackberry tree, Casey wondered what she would do if Fletcher refused to buy back a few acres of her property. Would she have the nerve to sell Robbins land to an outsider? No, she couldn't do that to Mack or Fletcher. But she couldn't disappoint John and Susan, either.

Casey stiffened at the slight movement of the cane pole in her hand. Her fingers tightened their grip on the slender shaft, then relaxed as she wrinkled her nose with indifference and decided to let this fish be the one that got away. Another yank of the line, stronger this time, brought a frown to her face. That fish was begging to be snagged, she argued. It must be a big one, too. Casey waited, muscles tense, for the next show of strength. When it came, she swept the hat from her head and tossed it aside, then jerked the line as she scrambled to her feet. Lurching forward, she froze and blinked in confusion at Fletcher, his eyes full of smug amusement as he held the line in her hand.

Hot color flooded her cheeks and prickled her ears before irritation replaced her embarrassment. She tossed the pole to the ground and bent to retrieve her hat. Dusting it against her thigh, Casey shoved the hat onto her head and turned to Fletcher with a glacial stare. But there was no way she could sustain the ice.

Did the man have any idea—any idea at all—how maddeningly attractive he was in that polo shirt, the way it stretched across his huge chest, faithfully outlining every muscle? There was nothing in his casual stance—hands on hips, feet slightly apart—that suggested he was aware of how his jeans molded the contours of his thighs so seductively. When his hands moved to slide into his back pockets, pulling the jeans tighter across his stomach, she drew in a deep breath.

"What are you doing here, Fletcher?"

"I need help, Casey. Last night I dreamed I was a tuna." He said it so seriously that for a moment she could only look into his blue-gray eyes then, refusing to let the smile that was playing at the corners of her mouth turn into a grin, she sat on the grass and rolled down the legs of her jeans.

"That's not such a problem, Fletcher. Make that a barracuda, and you'll be right on the money."

92

"Why, Casey, you cut me to the quick." His voice was full of mock dejection. "I think I deserve more than that after driving all this way."

"One of these days you'll get *exactly* what you deserve, Fletcher Robbins."

"Ah, hope springs eternal."

"Shut up and sit down."

"Good comeback, Casey."

She sighed with exasperation as he joined her on the grass. His easy smile and the relaxed look in his eyes told Casey that he was obviously in good spirits today. Surprising, when she considered their last bitter encounter. Still, she counted her blessings and weighed her chances of striking a deal with him.

"Why did you come, Fletcher?"

"Would you believe that I couldn't go another minute without basking in the sweet fragrance of your hair?" He leaned closer, and Casey shrank back.

"Try again. I smell like fish."

He breathed deeply and sighed. "To a tuna it's heaven."

This time she couldn't suppress the laughter, the sheer delight of seeing him again. With supreme effort she managed to still the rumblings of desire that began in her stomach and threatened to spread to all parts of her body. "You still haven't answered the question."

Fletcher leaned back on his elbows, staring with amused patience. "I try and I try, but you just will not be charmed, will you?" Actually, she was charmed to her toes. "I had to go to Bay City yesterday on business. On the way back this morning I decided to stop here and give you a ride home. Does that ease your suspicious female mind?"

She smiled an apology, touched that he had thought of her. "Now that you're here, there's something I'd like to discuss with you. It's about my land."

"What about it?"

"I'd like to sell some of it. Just a few acres."

The amusement flickered and died in his eyes. His expression became very serious . . . deadly serious. When he spoke his voice was cold and distant. "Do you have a buyer?" She looked away, regretting even the mention of the subject. His abrupt change of mood puzzled her thoroughly. What else could she do but forge ahead?

"Do you?" he demanded.

"Not yet. I was hoping you'd be interested." Swallowing with effort, she waited for his reply. When none came, she shifted her gaze from his brown leather boots to his sinewy thighs, outlined in blue denim, then up past the broad expanse of his chest to meet his steady, cold eyes.

"Why do you want to sell it, Casey? Does the land mean so little to you?"

She winced inside. "I appreciate what I have, if that's what you mean. I just need some cash for an investment."

"I could lend you—"

"No, Fletcher." Casey reached for her sandals and rose. "Are you interested in the land or not?"

Running his fingers through his hair, he stood and faced her. "You know damn well I am, but I can tell you this right now. I won't stop at a few acres. It's all or nothing."

"But, Fletcher, I don't—"

"All or nothing." This time he emphasized each word, imprinting them on her brain so there could be no room for doubt. "I'll pay you top dollar for the whole section."

The finality of his tone was infuriating. "Fletcher, I told you I don't want to sell it all."

"Why not?" he shot back with an accusing stare. "The land is neglected now. I can't do a damn thing with a few acres. But with a whole section I can graze a good-size herd and make it productive again. And best of all, I won't have you pestering me every time you need cash for some idiotic investment."

Pester. For a moment she was stunned by his cold remark. She wanted to hurt him as he had hurt her. "It would serve you right if I kept the land and set up housekeeping right under your nose," she said quietly.

"But you won't do that, will you?" he challenged. "You need cold, hard cash. And frankly, I'm beginning to think I wouldn't like you much as a neighbor, anyway. We can discuss the details on the drive back to the ranch."

"I have a reservation on the evening *flight,*" she said, lifting her chin in defiance.

"Cancel it."

"I will not!" Her heart pounded with anger at his heavy-handed attitude.

"Cancel the reservation or cancel the deal." Only the chill in his voice betrayed his controlled determination. "Now, if you'll excuse me, I've promised to help my nephews make some stilts." He turned to leave as if there couldn't possibly be anything more to say.

"Don't you think that's a *father's* responsibility?" The words were out before she knew it, and Casey regretted them just as quickly. She saw his shoulders stiffen as he turned back to her with eyes so full of disgust that Casey felt her body grow weak with remorse.

"You never gave me any children, Casey. Since this may be the closest I'll ever come to fatherhood, I intend to enjoy it to the fullest. Any objections?" He didn't wait for an answer. His easy strides carried him up the grassy knoll and out of her sight.

An impotent, whispered "No" was all she could manage.

Casey leaned back against the rich leather upholstery of Fletcher's car and kept her eyes on the seemingly endless ribbon of asphalt ahead. Only her purse separated her and Fletcher, but Casey realized with numbing despair that their spirits were so far apart that nothing could ever bridge the gap. Lunch at Susan's had been almost unbearable. Mercifully there had been no mention of fishing boats or real estate. Showering his charm and wit on Susan, John, and their sons, Fletcher had ignored her completely, as he did now.

She knew she had wounded him deeply with her callous remark and thought once about apologizing, but the words seemed so empty. Casey closed her eyes and sighed. Nothing she could say would erase the bitterness that crept into his eyes each time he looked her way.

God, he had made her so angry, though. Giving orders, delivering ultimatums, and making her feel guilty about selling her own land. They couldn't be together for five minutes without arguing. But that was no excuse for what she had said. How could she have hurt the man she—*still* cared for so much? The sudden realization of her feelings stabbed at her heart and deepened her conviction that Fletcher had always brought out both the best and the worst in her.

"Casey?" Fletcher's whisper opened her eyes, and she looked around her, aware that the quiet humming of the engine had ceased.

Why had he pulled off the road? she wondered. Then, viewing the wide expanse of white sand that spread before her eyes, Casey felt her knees grow weak as her mind's cry of anguish echoed through her.

"Remember this place?"

She nodded. How could she ever forget? Her gaze rested on the foamy white waves that taunted the shore, only to recede to the depths of the sparkling blue sea she remembered so well. She had tried to forget, thought she had succeeded in burying the bittersweet memories deep within the secret recesses of her mind. Casey had been certain they would never surface to hurt her again. But they did now, with invincible strength, tugging at her heart, forcing her to think back to the sultry moonlit night when, on this beach, Fletcher had made love to her for the first time.

It might have been any other stretch of beach along the Texas Gulf Coast, if not for the cozy white cottage that sat just out of reach of the drifting sand. In that house, he had made his simple declaration of love, then swam with her in the shimmering moonlight. When their desire for each other consumed them, Fletcher had drawn her to him on the wet sand and kissed away her every doubt about his feelings for her. She had laid bare every facet of her love for him, and he had received her feelings with reverent tenderness.

Casey clenched her fists. She had never wanted to come back here. Fletcher had asked her to do so many times, but she had always refused, preferring to keep their time here a special memory, cluttered with no others to dim its beauty or shadow its importance.

"Let's go for a walk." He was already out of the car.

"Fletcher, I'd rather not stay."

"Just for a few minutes. I'd like to stretch my legs."

You could do that anywhere but here! her mind screamed. When he came around to open the door, her eyes pleaded with him to let her forgo the ordeal. He ignored her silent request and took her hand to pull her from the car.

Casey slipped off her sandals and tossed them onto the floor of the Continental, then closed the door.

Looks never worked with Fletcher, she reminded herself as her toes sank into the sand. Only words. Words could have told him that she was afraid of her feelings about this place, that she didn't want to open the wounds and make them raw again. He would think her protests were weak and silly, though. Obviously, he had no such qualms about coming here. Well, if he didn't want to stay too long, she could survive it, too.

The ocean breeze whipped her raven hair about her face as she walked beside Fletcher toward a small delapidated boat dock. Thick ropes, frayed by time, lay scattered on the deck, their tattered ends swishing freely with the wind.

Tears gathered in her eyes, but Casey blinked them back in favor of a smile tinged with sadness. A memory, precious in its simplicity, filled her throat. Fletcher had chased her on that dock . . . chased her . . . and caught her. He had tickled her until, squealing with laughter, she had begged for mercy. And when he gave it, she pulled him along to the edge where, clinging to each other, they had toppled into the sea. She looked away. Her eyes aching with regret, she remembered how they had loved each other, caressed and held each other. Their bodies pressed into the silky wet sand on the shoreline, they had merged with each other to the deep rhythm of the sea and the shifting of the moonlight on the water. And later, in the bedroom of the small white house, the intensity of her own response—the passion Fletcher inspired in her—was enough to drown out even the thundering sound of the waves breaking on the rocky shore. So close. As close as two people could ever be; that's how she and Fletcher had been. She would never know that rare kind of intimacy again, not with any other man. She was sure of it. Why did they stop here? She had known it would be this way . . . poignant . . . painful.

Stopping to sit on a large piece of driftwood, Casey rested her chin in her palms and closed her eyes to a lone sailboat that rose and fell with the waves. The scent of Fletcher's after-shave mingled with the salty air, and she caught her breath, knowing he was near.

"This place has special meaning for us, Casey."

"Yes."

"Then, why are your eyes closed to the memories?"

She straightened and matched his steady gaze above her. Longing to smooth his unruly hair, she sighed and turned away. "Sometimes it's better that way, Fletcher. Like when I was a little girl, going through the fun house at the fair. All logic told me there was nothing to fear, but I was still afraid. So I closed my eyes and refused to feel, refused to think. Sometimes it's best just to close your mind and get through it."

"You're not a little girl anymore."

"No, but Fletcher, there are still a lot of things to get through."

"Is that how you felt about our divorce?"

The muscles around her eyes tensed at the pain of the memory. Casey forced them to relax as she shrugged. "In a way, I suppose. Although, you made it easier by not even showing up in court. There were no phone calls with bitter recriminations; no letters, begging me to come back. I wanted nothing, and yet you gave me the land and the Scout."

"You could've had more."

Casey sighed. "I know. At the time, though, I only wanted out. I wanted my life settled with some kind of future in sight."

"Was our marriage that bad, Casey?"

"Who knows?" She saw the bitterness in his eyes and knew he was searching for answers—answers that she couldn't give him. "Time blurs memories, Fletcher. Moments fade and we're left with only the feelings of the moment, not knowing what caused them." She looked down at the swirling grains of sand caught in the breeze at her feet. "I have to admit that, at times, I've wondered if things were as bad as they seemed, if what I felt—" She swallowed, unwilling to let him see the tears that blurred her vision.

"How did you feel? Go on and say it, Casey."

"No." She rose, her body trembling with resentment as she walked away. She couldn't answer any more of his probing questions. He had no right to ask them. Steadying her weak legs, she turned back to him. "It's all in the past, Fletcher. Why dredge it up again? There's no need."

"I suppose you're right." Fletcher leaned against the wooden piling of the deck. "I only hoped you'd be ready to explain about—you and Steve."

"Explain what? You wanted no explanation *then*. Why now? When it doesn't even matter." She jumped at the sudden slam of his fist on the piling.

"Damn it, Casey! Maybe I'm a masochist. Maybe I like having my ego crushed."

The hurt in his eyes leaped out at her, and Casey felt the tears forming in hers again.

With a sigh he rubbed the back of his head. "Or maybe now I'm man enough to—I don't know." His hand dropped to his side. "Forget it. Let's go home."

She watched him walk back to the car, then followed with labored steps. Had he brought her here to rid himself of the memories, the doubts about their marriage? What did he want from her? Reassurance? A guarantee that the same thing wouldn't happen to him with some other woman?

Opening the door, she sat in the car and stared ahead. Loneliness engulfed her. Fletcher was there, not two feet away, and she couldn't reach out to him. He wasn't hers anymore. Perhaps he never had been. He wanted Priscilla now. Didn't he know? Couldn't he sense how much she, Casey, needed him? Not to make love. She didn't want only that. Not really. She only wanted him to take her in his arms to hold her, to warm her, to make the loneliness go away.

"Casey, did you ever want children?" Fletcher asked quietly.

Her heart sank. He would insist on an answer, and she couldn't find the words to tell him all her feelings.

"Well, did you?" he goaded.

"I don't suppose I ever gave it much thought," she lied. Why this? Why now? Running her fingers through her hair, she took a deep breath and turned to him. "Look, why bring up things that are better off left in the past, that can only open a lot of old wounds . . . that should be forgotten? Let's just remember the wonderful moments we shared." Quietly she asked, "Remember how we used to dance?"

He turned away and stared out at the night in silence. "Then let's go dancing," he answered finally.

She smiled at him and locked his eyes firmly with hers. "There's a new country-and-western disco in Corpus. Take me dancing there, Fletcher. Let's be friends again."

"Fine," he answered slowly. Then he looked directly into her eyes. "If that's what you want."

"It is. It *is* what I want. Anything to stop all this talk about the past."

"Someday you'll have to face it, Casey," he said with a warning glance.

Not today, she thought, lifting her chin. There would be so little time with him. She wanted *new* memories to take with her when she left. Memories that would last the rest of her life.

CHAPTER SIX

As soon as the cocktail waitress took Fletcher's order and left, Casey turned her chair toward the dance floor and ignored Priscilla's reproving stare. The din of the lively country-and-western music made casual conversation difficult, and Casey counted herself lucky as she watched several couples, dressed in jeans and fringed western shirts, move around the dance floor.

At least I fit in with the crowd, she thought, silently taking inventory of her jeans, plaid shirt, and brown leather boots; but the disco, if it could be called that, was hardly the place she had imagined. The seedy-looking bar had absolutely nothing to recommend it except the good music, and even that was marred by poor acoustics. But she had insisted on coming here, she reminded herself ruefully.

Glancing across the table, she caught Fletcher's questioning stare and flashed him a defiant smile. She wasn't about to admit her mistake to him. He had caused her enough irritation already. She had worked hard all week at the blasting sites and now, when she finally had the chance to relax and enjoy an evening out with Fletcher, she had chosen a place like this. To top it off, Fletcher had invited Priscilla to come with them, and Casey wouldn't have been at all surprised if he had known all along about the second-story club with "early ghetto" decor.

Her only consolation was that Mack had agreed to join the party. His presence and the fact that Priscilla obviously loathed the place made Casey feel a little better.

The congenial smile on Mack's face as he tapped his foot in time with the music told Casey that he, at least, was enjoying himself. But then Mack could have a good time anywhere, she supposed. Pushing her straw hat farther back on her head, she resolved to follow his lead and make the best of the evening. When the waitress returned with a tray of drinks, Casey sipped her margarita and tried not to smile as Priscilla took a tissue from her purse to wipe the rim of her glass.

"Fletcher, I think we should have one drink, then leave," Priscilla said nervously, fingering the buttons of her black dinner dress.

"Since this was Casey's idea, I think she should decide when to leave." With smug amusement Fletcher patted Priscilla's hand, and Casey silently accepted his subtle challenge.

"Wait a minute," Mack interjected. "What's wrong with this place?"

"I don't like sleazy bars," Priscilla snapped.

Mack's smile widened into a chuckle as he shook his head. "I love 'em!" Then he sighed. "Loosen up, Priscilla. Have a few drinks, and we'll trip the light fantastic."

"I'm not moving from this chair until it's time to go home," Priscilla vowed, then pursed her lips, frowning.

"Suit yourself." Mack shrugged and rose. "Come on, Casey. Let's show them how the cotton-eyed Joe is done."

Casey hardly had time to set her drink on the table before she felt herself being pulled toward the dance floor.

It took no time at all to discover that Mack had never danced the cotton-eyed Joe. Although his boots came down on hers a few times, Casey ignored her wincing toes and joined in his contagious merriment.

Like a marathon dancer, unwilling to give up, Mack kept her on the dance floor through several songs, and by the time he finally escorted her back to the table, Casey's sagging spirits were thoroughly revitalized. She felt exhilarated and carefree. The momentary sense of abandonment she experienced when Mack left the table in search of other dance partners disappeared when she heard the whisper of a Texas twang in her ear.

"Would you like to dance?"

Ignoring Fletcher's warning glance, Casey smiled and rose. "I'd love—to." She stared at a huge male chest. As her gaze traveled up past the man's meaty neck to the puffy cheeks of his face, images of a bulldog flashed through Casey's mind. His twinkling blue eyes reassured her only a little, but she decided that one dance wouldn't kill her.

For someone who outweighed her by at least a hundred and fifty pounds, the big man with the ten-gallon hat was amazingly light on his feet, Casey thought as he whirled her around the dance floor.

"Just grab my belt loop and hang on," he said. "You come here much?"

A breathless "No" was all she could manage.

"My name's Billy, but most folks just call me Bruiser. What's your handle?"

She blinked in confusion before she recognized his trucker jargon. "Casey," she replied, concentrating on the fast dance steps.

"That man at the table your husband?"

Again a "No" escaped her lips, and Casey realized her

mistake as Bruiser tightened his hold on her. "He's a good friend, though," she quickly added.

When the music stopped, Casey thanked him and turned to walk back to her seat. She felt his huge, rough hand pulling her back to his side.

"Let's go another round," he suggested.

"Maybe later, Bruiser."

Still, he held her hand.

"I believe you promised this next dance to me, Casey." She sighed with relief at the sound of Fletcher's deep drawl. Smiling an apology to Bruiser, Casey turned to Fletcher's outstretched arms.

"Okay, but I'll be back," Bruiser called as Fletcher swept her to another part of the floor. His big hand closed in a perfect fit over her small one while his other arm wrapped itself tenderly around her waist.

At first she kept a casual distance, but Fletcher's tight lips made it clear that he didn't appreciate her efforts at Platonism. She was sure he would have, had he known the control it took to keep her breasts from melting into his hard chest the way they had at other times ... times when he had loved her. With a single nudge he pulled her against him.

"There," he said with finality, as though now their dance could really begin. She smiled delightedly into his shoulder, letting her lips press against the yoke of his shirt, remembering all the times he had held her like this. She could once again feel the warmth of his skin under her fingertips, the firmness of his thighs grazing smoothly against hers, the slight tremor of his chest against her breasts. She let her hands roam across the suppleness of his broad back, finally resting on his slim hips as she pulled him closer to her.

"Casey, why did you dance with him?" The irritation in his voice made her stiffen.

She shrugged. "Somebody had to. I can handle him, Fletcher. Besides, Bruiser's a nice enough man," she said defensively.

"Bruiser? My God, his name alone should tell you what kind of man he is."

"Well, he has nice eyes."

"He has *glazed* eyes, Casey. He's drunk. You've had your fun. Now, let's go home." Fletcher stopped dancing.

"I'm not ready," she flared and matched his icy stare. "I'm sure Priscilla can't wait to leave, can she? Why did you ask her to come, anyway?"

"I didn't ask her. . . ." Fletcher's words trailed off as his eyes focused on a point somewhere above her head.

Casey turned to see Bruiser smiling down at her.

"I'm back," he said smoothly.

"She's all yours, *Bruiser.*" With a challenging glance at Casey, Fletcher released her and walked back to the table.

She fumed inside when she saw Fletcher lean close to Priscilla in obvious intimate conversation, but Bruiser allowed her no time for further ponderance. He pulled her into the circle of his beefy arms and swung her around the floor several times until she thought she might collapse if he didn't stop.

"Bruiser, I think I should join my friends now," she told him.

"Don't worry about them. They're gone." His cheeks puffed into a wide grin.

Her heart sank as she whirled around to discover that her table was now occupied by strangers.

Oh, my God! her mind raced. *Surely Fletcher wouldn't leave me in this place alone.*

"Come on, Casey. The music started again." Bruiser grabbed her hand.

"I don't want to dance anymore."

His beefy features sagged with disappointment, but then

he quickly rallied. "Okay, how about a game of eight ball?" Before she could decline, he pushed her through the crowd to the back of the club, where a pool table stood beneath the glow of a bar lamp. As Bruiser racked the balls, then handed her a cue stick, Casey stared at the green felt of the table and searched her mind for the best way to handle him. She decided to play one game, then sneak off to the ladies' room and call somebody—anybody.

"Break 'em up, sweetie."

She smacked the cue ball with contempt and watched the cluster of balls at the other end of the table spin out of their triangular formation. Each time Casey shot another ball with unwavering accuracy into one of the pockets, she noticed that Bruiser's attitude became a little more surly. He left her side only to take his turn or order another beer, then slipped to her elbow again.

"Eight ball in the side pocket," Casey said, when the game neared its end. She knew she should lose this match to spare Bruiser's ego, but her pride and a certain reckless urge for revenge wouldn't allow that. The black eight ball rolled slowly to the pocket and disappeared inside it.

"Let's play again. No broad is going to beat me at pool or anything else." The slur of his words told Casey that she had waited much too long to leave.

"Find another partner, Bruiser. I'm going home." She smiled nervously.

"Uh-uh." He shook his head as his eyes narrowed into slits of blue. When he edged around the pool table toward Casey, she backed away in panic.

Before she knew it her hand curled around the cue ball and she picked it up, hoping the mere threat would give him pause. Casey knew by the look in his eyes, though, that Bruiser would not be dissuaded. There was only one thing to do, she decided, hurling the ball at his chest. The ball ricocheted off his shoulder and back to the table. Casey watched the white ball bounce once, then roll to a halt. She looked around at the nameless faces of the few men who stood close by, shuffling and mumbling among themselves.

Fletcher, damn it! Where are you? her mind screamed.

As Bruiser swaggered closer Casey instinctively raised her cue stick. Bruiser grabbed the stick from her hand, then snapped it across his thigh, and Casey's heart pounded with terror. She licked her dry lips and searched her mind for something witty to say that would make this man back away from her. His gaze never left her face as he raised thick, hairy hands to her shoulders.

"Ready to go now, Casey?" Fletcher asked, stepping between her and Bruiser to break the huge man's hold.

Staring at Fletcher's broad back, Casey almost fainted with relief, but she locked her knees and forced her legs to support her.

Fletcher would take care of this. She wasn't alone anymore. There was no need to be afraid. As her mind rattled off each thought in staccato rhythm, Casey stood on tiptoes to peek over Fletcher's shoulder. She saw Bruiser's huge hands curl into fists and wondered vaguely if Fletcher was ready for—

She stepped aside instinctively as she heard the resounding smack against Fletcher's jaw. She spun around to see him sprawled across a tabletop behind her. The two male customers who sat at the table expressed only mild surprise at the sudden intrusion. Without a word they glanced at each other and sprang from their chairs to shove Fletcher back into the arena. Casey stood in wide-eyed amazement when Fletcher seemed to catapult past her, his head bent low as it connected with Bruiser's midsection. The blow sent Bruiser reeling backward, knocking a few of the onlookers to the floor.

As if on cue, men who had moments ago seemed reluctant to help her now eagerly joined in the brawl while Casey looked on with open-mouthed shock. Men who seemed so peaceful began to sock each other with gusto, paying no attention to overturned chairs and broken glass. And Fletcher was right in the middle of it all!

"Oh, my God! This is magnificent!"

Mack's gruff voice sounded in her ears, and Casey's gaze swung to the bar to see him leaning against the dull wood. His twinkling eyes locked onto the scene before him as he signaled the bartender to serve him another drink. His excitement as he punched and jabbed at the air made Casey hurry to his side.

"Mack! Can't you do something?" The question was more of a command as Casey searched the flailing arms and legs of the mob for a glimpse of Fletcher. "Those men are so big!"

"I know. Isn't it great?" Mack grabbed her collar and hauled her to his other side just as one man crashed against the bar.

She stared in wonder at the spot she had vacated and watched the man sink slowly to the floor. The constant sound of hard knuckles connecting with soft flesh became a blur in Casey's mind as she continued her search for Fletcher's face in the crowd.

When she finally caught sight of him as he landed a right hook to Bruiser's ribs, beads of perspiration broke out on her forehead. Her fear was for Fletcher now, and Casey clenched her fists nervously, knowing she alone was responsible for the full-scale fight that unfolded before her. She winced at the sound of shattering bottles, then turned to Mack.

"We've got to get Fletcher out of here, Mack. Isn't there some way we can sneak him down the stairs and out to the street?"

Mack shook his head impatiently and waved her aside. "We'd have a better chance with a knotted bedsheet. The police will be here soon, anyway."

Just as he spoke the words, Casey heard the shrill blasts of whistles. She blinked her eyes into focus as the houselights burst to life and she saw uniformed men shove their way through the mob. Only a few diehards continued to pummel each other as the policemen separated the fighters. The moans and groans that rumbled through the now subdued crowd dwindled to whispers as Bruiser lay in a stupor across the pool table. Casey silently thanked the stars for his unconscious condition.

She looked around to see Fletcher coming toward her as he ran bruised fingers through his disheveled blond hair before covering his head with his hat. His shirt was torn and smudged, and the red, swollen gash on his cheek brought Casey's hand to her face as her own cheek stung with empathy.

Turning from Fletcher's disdainful gaze, she wondered fleetingly about proper etiquette in a situation like this. Were congratulations in order? Should she thank him for coming to her rescue? Casey knew what she *wanted* to do. She wanted to hold him and soothe him. She wanted him to return her embrace, to feel her regret, but his mocking stare pinned her arms to her sides as she swallowed in an attempt to rid herself of the guilt.

"Let's go home." Fletcher's words were directed to Mack, but his gaze remained on Casey.

"Wait just a minute—sir."

Casey and Fletcher turned at the same time to see a young khaki-clad policeman, looking slightly uncomfortable as he squared his broad shoulders and cleared his throat. "I've been told that you're responsible for starting this fight, sir."

110

Casey's gaze shifted from the policeman to Fletcher, then back again before she stepped between them.

"What are you talking about?" she asked indignantly. "He didn't start anything."

"Casey, let me handle this," Fletcher whispered through clenched teeth. He drew her to his side. "Officer, I'm sorry about all this. I'll be happy to pay for any damages."

"Nevertheless, I'm afraid you'll have to come with me."

"What?" Casey stepped between the two men again. "Officer, this man is innocent," she stated, jerking her thumb toward Fletcher. "He's the most honorable—Why, do you know who this man is?" Her hands rested on her hips as one foot tapped the floor impatiently.

"Yes, ma'am. I believe he's Fletcher Robbins," the officer replied.

"Hmph! If you know that, how could you possibly consider arresting him?"

"Casey, will you please get out of the way?" Fletcher pulled her aside again, this time gripping her arm firmly.

"Now, could you please tell me what happened, Mr. Robbins?" the officer continued, flipping open a black notebook.

"Don't tell him anything, Fletcher," Casey said, lifting her chin. Undaunted by Fletcher's painful squeeze on her arm, she directed an icy stare at the policeman. "He doesn't have to tell you anything without an attorney. Besides, he didn't start the fight."

"Is that true, Mr. Robbins?"

"That's true." Fletcher relaxed his grip and sighed.

"Then who did start the trouble?"

"Tell him, Fletcher," Casey commanded. Staring at the floor, she wondered smugly how many days Bruiser would spend in jail for trying to be such a ladies' man? An expressive silence brought her gaze up to Fletcher's finger,

111

pointed directly at her as he looked straight ahead. A lump rose in her throat.

"Fletcher, how could you? I didn't hit anyone!" She looked to the policeman. "Well, that's not exactly true. I did throw that one cue ball, but—well, I had to do something. I—"

"I think you'd *both* better come with me."

Against Fletcher's warning to the contrary, Casey rambled on in a daze with her explanation as the policeman led her downstairs and outside to the patrol car, its red light rotating with authority. Almost before she knew it she was seated beside Fletcher in the backseat. Two officers deposited themselves in front as Casey heard the engine start. She sank low to avoid the curious stares of passing pedestrians.

God, how humiliating, she thought, then suddenly remembered Mack. Her irritation returned as she straightened her posture and lifted her chin.

"Mack didn't even try to help us, Fletcher."

"The smartest move he ever made," Fletcher said dryly. "Besides, we'll need someone to bail us out."

"You're an attorney," she snapped. "Can't you do it?"

"No, I can't. An attorney can't go his own bail."

Casey swallowed with effort. "Well, I'm sure Mack will come. Priscilla—where's Priscilla?"

"She was waiting outside when the fight broke out. Mack will take her home before he comes after us."

"Hmph. It's a pity you couldn't have stayed put at the table while I was dancing. Maybe none of this would have happened."

"It's a pity I didn't stuff you in a burlap bag and drag you out of there," Fletcher returned. "Instead, I let you *handle* things."

Ignoring his remark, she studied her faint reflection in

112

the window. "What charges do you think will be brought against us when we get to the police station?"

"Oh, they'll probably get you on assault with a sharp tongue and a round weapon. It may be attempted murder for me."

"My God!" She gasped and turned to him. "Fletcher, you haven't killed anyone!"

He shot her a dark look. "Yet."

"Cute," she said, wrinkling her nose. "I'm sure the police will understand when I tell them how Bruiser was leering at me."

"Oh, he's sure to get life for that."

"Just stop it," she demanded through tight lips. "This is all so embarrassing for me and—"

"Embarrassing for *you?*" He shook his head with restrained astonishment. "I'm almost forty years old, Casey. I've just been involved in a rumble. Do you hear that, Casey?" His face came closer to hers, and she stiffened as his words grew more intense. "A supposedly mature, upstanding citizen who, at the moment, hurts right down to his eyelashes, has been involved in a barroom brawl and is now on his way to jail. All because you didn't have the good sense to say no to a drunk." He turned her face to him. "So I really don't care to hear about your embarrassment. Just shut your mouth and let me do the talking from now on."

She jerked her chin away from his hand as her breasts heaved. "You can rest assured that I'll *never* speak to you again."

"You're just saying that to make me feel better," he said, raking his fingers impatiently through his hair.

"You two want to hold it down back there?" the young officer called over his shoulder. "We can't hear the calls on our radio."

Casey bit back her few choice words for the officer.

113

Closing her eyes, she wished desperately that the rest of the evening would go in fast-forward motion and morning would find the nightmare over.

"Oh, Fletcher, I've been so worried!" Priscilla flung herself against Fletcher's chest as Casey and Mack steadied him. "I came over as soon as I heard." Priscilla took Fletcher's arm. Casting a reproachful glance toward Casey, Priscilla led him to the sofa.

Casey slumped to the easy chair and watched the scene with despairing resignation as Priscilla leaned over Fletcher and patted his cheek.

"You poor darling. It must have been awful for you."

"Awful? It was *fantastic!*" Mack stated, stepping to the bar. "Priscilla, you missed a whoppin' good time. I just wish you could've been there to see Fletcher in action." Mack shook his head with pride, then stopped to eye the pitcher of clear liquid on the bar. "What's this? Martinis to welcome us home from the war?"

"That's lemonade," Priscilla replied tersely. "I thought Fletcher might like some after the ordeal he's been through." She filled a glass and set it on the table beside Fletcher. "Now, I'll get some antiseptic for that nasty cut."

When she left the room, Mack hurriedly added a few jiggers of vodka to the pitcher, then poured himself a glassful. "Casey, would you like some?"

She smiled and declined with a shake of her head. At least Priscilla would never tame *him,* she thought gratefully, but Fletcher was another story. He hadn't spoken to her on the drive home, but Casey sensed his anger had abated somewhat. At least he hadn't scowled at her for the past few minutes. If there were only something she could do, some peaceful gesture that would show her regret.

Casey rose and walked to the bar. Unfolding a white

linen napkin, she filled the center with crushed ice, then wrapped the cloth around it. Crossing the room, she gently placed the ice pack on Fletcher's cheek. He flinched at first, but then relaxed as his hand covered hers. For a moment her gaze met his, and Casey saw the questioning look in his eyes. How this man could melt her with a single look; it simply wasn't fair.

"I thought the ice might take the swelling down," she offered, lowering her lashes.

"I can do that, Casey." Priscilla, armed with gauze and antiseptic, entered the room and sat beside Fletcher. "I think you've done quite enough damage for one evening. That cut needs to be cleaned."

Casey slipped her hand from beneath Fletcher's and walked back to her chair. It wouldn't do to cause another scene, she decided, choking back her anger. Casey winced as the first dabs of alcohol touched Fletcher's skin. He grabbed Priscilla's wrist and held it away from his face.

"The ice feels better."

"I know, darling, but there's no telling what kind of germs you might have picked up in a place like that."

"I've had all my shots, Priscilla. I probably won't start foaming at the mouth for another fifteen minutes." Fletcher rose and added vodka to his lemonade.

"By the way, there was an on-the-scene report on the ten o'clock news," Priscilla replied. "*Dear* Mack told them everything."

"Come back here, Mack." The edge in Fletcher's voice brought Casey's head up to see her ex-father-in-law sidling toward the door.

"Now, Fletcher," Mack began, turning around slowly. "The interview I gave that reporter was all very low-key and dignified."

"I'll bet. What did he say, Priscilla?" Fletcher's eyes remained on Mack.

115

"He was very cooperative," Priscilla said, obviously taking great satisfaction from seeing Mack squirm. "He told the reporters how his son was on the boxing team in college."

"Background information," Mack said gruffly, glancing around the room.

"And I thought his blow-by-blow account of the fight was most colorful." Priscilla smiled thinly as she rose and stood beside Fletcher. "Really, Mack. How could you have done such a stupid thing?"

Casey's hands gripped the arms of her chair as she pushed herself to her feet. "Why don't you take your foot off his throat, Priscilla? So, he gave an interview. I think it's lucky the press heard the story from Mack, who probably told it with a sense of humor, rather than from someone who might try to blow it all out of proportion."

"If that's the way you feel, then you won't mind what he said about you," Priscilla countered with an acid stare. "Mack told the whole state of Texas that this isn't the first time Fletcher has had to defend your—honor. A bullfighter in Mexico City, wasn't it?"

A hot wave of embarrassment engulfed Casey as she closed her eyes and shook her head in disbelief, then looked askance at Mack. "You really make it hard for a person to come to your defense."

"Now, Casey." Mack scratched the back of his head. "All I said was that some bullfighter got out of hand, and Fletcher had to deck him. That's all."

"Yes, I'm sure you found the whole evening great fun, Mack." Priscilla walked to the patio doors, then turned around, her arms folded across her breasts. "You don't seem to realize what an embarrassment you are to Fletcher. I, for one, think you made a complete fool of yourself."

"Think again." Casey's lips trembled with rage as her

116

heart pounded. No one could say those things to Mack and get away with it.

"I'll *think* whatever I like," Priscilla snapped. "If Fletcher wasn't so upset already, I'd give you both a piece of my mind."

Anger writhed inside Casey, but she forced her voice to remain calm. "Oh, come on, Priscilla. Are you sure you can spare it?"

"Casey!"

At Fletcher's sharp reprimand, her gaze clashed with his disbelieving stare. Slowly their thoughts blended into silent agreement that *he* would set Priscilla straight.

"Mack, it's been a long evening." Casey walked to his side and linked her arm in his. "Why don't we get a good night's sleep?"

As they climbed the stairs together Casey yielded to the urge to reassure him. "Mack, Fletcher will make sure Priscilla never says anything like that again."

"I know." The quiet confidence in his voice made her turn to fathom the look in his twinkling eyes before his lashes lowered to veil the humor.

"Mack, you rotten rascal! You staged this whole thing, didn't you?"

"No. I just took advantage of some amazing opportunities, but if you tell Fletcher, I'll deny it to my dying breath." After planting a kiss on her numb cheek, he left her staring blankly in the hallway.

Thoughts of Fletcher bombarded her mind as she made her way through her own room to the adjoining bath and turned on the tap. Undressing, she shivered to think of Fletcher's reaction should he ever learn of Mack's shenanigans. To put it mildly, Fletcher wouldn't be happy to know that Mack had baited Priscilla, then reeled her in on a line that clearly showed her disdain for Mack and her possessiveness of Fletcher. Casey sighed as the warm bubbles drifted around her body in the tub.

It's not my problem, she reminded herself. Mack had proven himself to be more than a match for Priscilla, and if his son wasn't discerning enough to see that Priscilla wasn't right for him, well . . . he would learn, hopefully, before it was too late. She punctuated the thought with a stab at a bubble, then sank lower into the water.

Disturbed by the things she had learned about herself that evening, Casey wrinkled her nose. During the brawl and afterward she had surprised herself with the primitive instincts that had risen within her. At first she was appalled at the mere thought of Fletcher in a fight; but tingling pride began to hover around the edges of her mind and, no matter how much she chided herself for the feeling, her secret delight couldn't be denied.

Did all women feel that way? Casey wondered. That same delicious exultation at being protected by a man? Scooping a handful of bubbles into her palm, she blew them back to the water and suppressed the urge to snicker. She supposed she had felt that way in Mexico City too, when Fletcher had punched a man for becoming too familiar with her. She had all but forgotten the incident and silently thanked Mack for the reminiscence.

Casey closed her eyes and sighed, realizing that she wouldn't have felt the same at just any man's protection. Only Fletcher's. Childish as it seemed, he was her hero, in a way—her prince—the only one she had ever wanted to drench the desert of parched emotions within her.

Her emerald eyes fluttered open. She sat up . . . slowly. It wasn't a sound that betrayed Fletcher's presence . . . only her body's tingling awareness, beginning at the nape of her neck and gradually rippling to her toes. A flick of her gaze over his huge fully dressed body made her conscious—acutely so—of her own nudity. He rested

118

against the doorframe, his big hands curled around the two glasses he held. Any pretense of modesty was melted by the smoldering intensity of his eyes.

"How long have you been here, Fletcher?" she asked, basking in the delicious feelings that haunted her.

"Long enough for these tequila sunrises to turn into hot toddies," he replied in a raspy whisper.

She bit her lip and drew a quivery breath. "You might've said something . . . at least cleared your throat."

"I couldn't. My heart was in it." His lips curved to a sensuous smile, and Casey moaned inwardly, dragging her gaze back to the water.

An ambiance of tantalizing danger pervaded the room. The power to excite him, the pleasure of pleasing him, filled her with daring temptation. She wanted him to watch . . . to see . . . to enjoy . . . and knew his admiration would fuel—as it always had—the desire that purred inside her.

Fletcher did watch . . . and see . . . and enjoy . . . the damp ringlets that clung to her luscious neck, the upward tilt of her breasts with rosy nipples just visible above the bubbles. But when she slowly rose from the water and stood before him, white clouds of foam sliding the length of her wet, silky thighs, he ached with a need to go forth and touch her . . . touch the satin-smooth skin of her flat stomach, her full hips. Instead, he pressed his shoulder hard against the wood on which he had only leaned a moment ago. She needed time, and he would wait as long as he could. His eyes narrowed at the pert lift of her chin as she wrapped the towel around her.

Casey trembled inside as she tucked the velour at her breasts. With faltering steps she walked toward him and took the glass he offered.

"I just wanted to share a drink with my partner in crime," he said softly.

"You're not angry anymore?" Her fingers tightened around the glass.

He shook his head. "No."

As her drink slipped from her hand Fletcher caught it and set the glass on the vanity. She shivered as his fingers began a slow, rhythmic movement from her shoulder to her elbow and back again.

"You know, with a little practice we could knock over two or three bars a week," he said, looking into her eyes.

"You mean—like Bonnie and Clyde?" she asked weakly.

"No, we couldn't start out in the big time right away, but I think it could be very profitable in the long run. I plan to sink all my money into barroom equipment. Glasses, chairs—the works."

"Oh, I see." Cocking an eyebrow, she shook her head knowingly. "Then I could go in and pick out the biggest brute in the bar, then ply him with liquor—but actually, I'd be casing the joint all the time."

"Exactly. Then I'd come in and bust up the place. They'd be forced to buy new equipment. We'd make a killing in no time."

"Sounds interesting." Her strength dwindled to almost nothing as she felt his arms go around her waist, but she forced herself to continue the game. "Mack could drive the getaway car."

"No, Mack couldn't handle that. He'd spill his guts to the ten o'clock news. Let's just keep this between you and me," he said with a wink.

"Whatever you say." She was ready to do anything he asked, if only he would ask.

Her heart began to pound in expectation as he led her into the bedroom and turned her to him. His kiss was light but expressive, sending shock waves of longing through her.

"Casey, I want to make love to you."

Her lips quivered a sigh as she drew him closer and stood on tiptoes, resting her cheek against the warmth of his neck. Electric energy flowed between them as she clung to him. "Could I wear the top to your pajamas?" she asked, thinking back to glorious days and nights spent in his arms.

"Later. I'd only have to take it off again."

She lifted her face to his. "But I like—"

"I know what you like," he said in a voice that compelled her lips to his.

Then his mouth covered hers with soft assurance that rekindled her aching desire and set it spiraling through her veins. The towel fell away, and she stiffened, then relaxed as his expert hands began a slow exploration of her curves.

She also succumbed to her ravenous need to know every inch of him again. She tugged each side of his shirt from the waist of his jeans. One by one, she unfastened the pearl snaps, celebrating each triumph with a tender kiss on his hair-covered chest. When he shrugged out of his shirt, she dropped it to a chair and stepped into his arms again, aching with the knowledge that she couldn't bear to be kept away too long. With a groan of pleasure he held her, his lips moving over her cheeks and eyes until she hungered for him . . . all of him.

She unbuttoned the studs of his jeans and slipped a trembling hand inside. A violent shiver ran the length of his magnificent body as she caressed the fire inside him.

When the rest of his clothes lay strewn about the carpet and his boots were set by the bedside table, he pulled her back to the breathless world he had created for her. His mouth coaxed her breasts to swelling, blazing peaks. His fingers traced her spine, then fanned out to cup her hips, setting them in seductive motion under his tantalizing direction. Her hands slipped up to encircle his neck, and she wanted to drown in his bewitching embrace. Each kiss he bestowed honed her senses, driving all thoughts, save him, from her mind.

When he lowered her to the bed, her quivering body was finely tuned to respond to his slightest touch. The sight of his naked, virile beauty filled her with an intense yearning to experience the total weight of him. She reached out to him, pulling him down to cover her completely with sensual possession. The rough-soft texture of his chest against her breasts stirred the love within her. This was the essence of Fletcher, the rough-soft golden man she had never been able to forget . . . the lusty man who had swept her back into his life once more.

His lips tasting her, his hands taunting her, every movement of his body drew her closer to the edge of ecstasy until her every nerve was strung tight, begging to be taken captive. Then, when she thought she would surely cry out from the sensations, he gathered her to him and slowly, agonizingly, began the age-old—ever new—love rhythm that makes man and woman one. Their bodies entwined with free, fiery emotions that swelled to a feverish pitch. Together they experienced an exquisite blending of white-hot energy that peaked and exploded with a rapturous, awesome force. She clung to him fiercely at first, then gradually relaxed her hold on his strong, throbbing body.

When her passion had receded to the shadowy depths from whence it sprang, she kissed him and smoothed the damp hair from his forehead. With a sigh of affection Casey shifted beneath the weight of his thigh across hers and rolled onto her side. He pulled her against him again, encircling her breasts with his possessive embrace.

"I've waited a long time to have you again," he whispered. "Don't try to leave me so soon."

His words brought a satisfied smile to her lips as she

closed her eyes and realized that she wanted never to leave his comforting arms again. Although she knew that daybreak would bring with it a measure of reason, tonight she would let hopes run rampant in dreams.

CHAPTER SEVEN

Casey lazily stretched her elbows above her head and blinked at the pale morning sunlight that bathed the room through open windows. Smiling at the sight of rose-colored draperies being teased by a soft breeze, she closed her eyes and snuggled deeper into Fletcher and the vivid memory of his scintillating kisses and caresses. Her fingers trailed his heavy, tanned forearm lying across her breasts as though, even in sleep, he refused to let her stray from his side. She reached for his hand and drew it to her lips, kissing his fingertips one by one before she molded them to the curve of her breast again.

Had time allowed, she would have gathered a Fletcher-scented pillow to her and lost herself in sleep again. But it was dawn, and she was due at the blasting site.

Reluctantly she wriggled her hips from beneath his warm thigh and placed his arm to rest at his side. She drank in the sight of his rakish, sun-streaked hair, contrasting sharply with the shadowy stubble of beard. In sleep his normally firm mouth was curved slightly as if it might smile at any moment. His nose was a thoroughly charming affair. Straight—but not rigidly so. His nostrils flared minutely with each slow breath he took. The gentle cleft of his chin softened the squareness of his firm jawline.

A loving ache in her throat almost consumed her, but Casey resisted the urge to wake Fletcher and relive the wonderful feelings, the glorious reconciliation she had shared with him. He looked too peaceful, too precious to disturb so early in the morning. Nonetheless, she let her fingers feather across the curly tangle of hair on his hard chest. With a tiny moan she bent toward him. Then, before his very existence changed her mind again, she planted a playful kiss on his nose and left him to shower and dress.

An impish smile curved her lips as she took his silk shirt from a chair and slipped her arms into the long sleeves, engulfing herself in his possession. Rolling the cuffs to her wrists, she tiptoed to the bath adjoining Fletcher's room so as not to disturb his sleep. Manly scents from masculine decanters left her feeling more feminine than she had in such a long time. Letting her fingers stroke the satiny smooth sleeve, she experienced a renewed appreciation of her ability to taste, touch, and feel. She admitted joyously that Fletcher was responsible for the reawakening.

As the cool spray of the shower pummeled energy into her body, reason began to filter through her dreamy thoughts.

She loved him.

There was no denying that now—not to herself, at least. Perhaps she had never stopped loving him. And though he hadn't said so in words, she guessed he must still feel something for her, too. *Don't think any further than that,* she told herself. But her knees trembled in stubborn rejection of the admonition. Fletcher would be away in San Antonio all day. When he returned, they would have to talk everything out, tell each other their feelings. The time until night seemed an eternity . . . until she considered the two years she'd been without him.

She had doubts, fears she longed to lay to rest. She thought of them all as she dressed in jeans and a red cotton shirt. Pulling a brush through her hair, she tied the black tresses with a ribbon at her nape and turned for one last look at Fletcher.

He had shifted to a sprawl on his stomach now. The hem of the white sheet touched just below his waist and hinted at a thoroughly muscled slope of one buttock, its appeal enhanced by the sun-bronzed glow of his back.

Shouldn't she at least leave a note telling him how much their night together had meant to her? She could pin it— With a stinging recollection Casey dismissed the idea before it was completely formed. Pinning a note to his pillow would surely be a painful reminder of the last note she had left him. No. Better to talk to him in person. Then, if there was any misunderstanding, she would *show* him how she felt . . . again and again.

The delightful anticipation of making love with Fletcher stayed with her as she drove toward the first blasting site on the day's schedule. Miles of fences with alternating wood and metal posts sped by as the Scout bounced over the dusty dirt road, flanked by athel trees. When she reached a large green pasture about ten miles north of the house, Casey drove the vehicle through a bump gate that closed behind her. Pungent smells of sagebrush and other summer vegetation drifted to her nostrils and reminded her once again how much she had missed the ranch during her absence.

The rolling, pitching movement of the Scout as it crossed the open field came to an end when Casey spotted a one-ton truck and an older model pickup parked side by side near an ebony tree. Of the several men who relaxed in the shade, the two who leaned against the pickup greet-

126

ed her affably when she slammed the door of the Scout and walked toward them.

She recognized a leathery-faced elderly man as Digger, a former roughneck turned blasting man, and Kevin, a young redheaded geology student who worked with the seismology crew during summer vacations. Both men were trusted employees of her company, and she was grateful they were available for this assignment.

"Hello, Digger. Kevin. It feels as though it's going to be another scorcher today, so why don't we get started?" Nodding to the rest of the crew, Casey opened her black notebook and began scanning the pages for information about this particular area.

At her instructions, Digger and Kevin took the other men and set out to deposit the explosives in more than a dozen shallow, predrilled holes scattered around the pasture. She stayed behind to assemble and adjust the equipment that would record the vibrations made by the blast.

As soon as the dynamite was planted at all the right coordinates, the men returned to the truck to wait for the detonation. When it came, the explosion jarred her feet as the earth erupted in a shower of rock and dirt.

Stunned, Casey blinked in confusion as she followed Digger's lead and made a quick dive beneath the pickup. Kevin joined her immediately, and she could only hope the rest of the crew had found shelter.

When the noise of the pelting rocks subsided, she crawled on her belly from beneath the truck to stand staring, first at Digger, then Kevin. The sheepish grin on the younger man's dust-grimed face made her sigh with irritation.

"Kevin, the force of the blast is supposed to go down, not up," she reminded him as she brushed the debris from her hair. "What happened? Didn't you pack the holes tight enough?"

"Apparently not." Kevin shrugged by way of apology.

"Well, no one got hurt," Digger said, dusting the dirt from his trousers. "Sometimes the holes just backfire and there's not much you can do about it."

"I know." Wouldn't Fletcher just love to come home to a cattle stampede? "Let's try it again, but this time remember this isn't Mount Vesuvius."

As the men fanned out in the pasture again Casey wiped a dun-colored film of dust from the seismograph, then sat in the shade of the ebony tree to wait for the next detonation.

This time the blast went as planned, the ground rumbling beneath her feet as Casey watched the needle on the seismograph record the vibrations and shock waves. When the needle ceased to move, she marked the exact location of the blasting site on the tape and stored it in a leather case for future inspection; then she would be able to examine thoroughly the squiggly lines and determine the slope of the subsurface rock formation.

By noon she and the crew had tested two more sites. Casey graciously declined Digger's invitation to lunch at one of the modern-day chuck wagons that traveled the range, serving the hungry cowpunchers employed by the ranch. She had no appetite for food, only solitude—time to think about Fletcher. She placed the morning's tapes on the seat beside her and started the motor.

Casey drove to the next site, a marshy area nestled between two rolling green ridges, and parked beside a shaded watering hole, one of the many artesian wells that had been drilled by Fletcher's ancestors. Dipping her handkerchief into the clear spring water, she spread the damp cloth over her face and felt her skin tingle with cool refreshment. She wrapped the handkerchief around her neck and sat at the edge of the water to enjoy her iced tea.

Serene, beautiful, rugged, she thought, looking out to

128

the open country. If her own land was only half as inspiring . . . but she couldn't remember much about the part of the ranch that belonged to her, except that it lay in the Santa Rosa division. She had only scanned the details of her divorce settlement. Closer examination had been too painful a task at the time of her court hearing. Besides, a legal description couldn't tell her the things she wanted to know. What kind of birds called from the trees? Was it rich farm land or rugged mesquite country like this?

Shading her eyes against the glare of the sun, she focused on a distant windmill that turned slowly with the breeze. Perhaps it wouldn't matter soon. Perhaps there would be no need to think about things like *his* land and *her* land, only two people's lives—together.

Casey shifted her gaze back to the spring and let the water trickle through her fingers, uncertainty trickling through her thoughts. Was she moving too fast? Was she allowing herself to get caught up in fantasy and impossible expectations? Thinking clearly had always been difficult whenever Fletcher made love to her the way he had the night before. Even now the memory of his tender eagerness, his sensuous hands moving over her, began to melt her powers of reason. It took all the will she possessed to ignore the vision of his passion-filled eyes, the seductive smile.

Of course she was happy about her feelings for him. But would he feel the same? They had loved each other before, and still their marriage had failed. There were no guarantees that it would work this time. Fletcher in his usual deliberation might not be so eager to rush into marriage again—at least not with her.

Resting her head against the trunk of an ebony tree, Casey remembered Mack's words the night of her arrival at the ranch. *The possibility of a wedding.* She frowned, the memory mingling with Fletcher's own comment that dependent women were a lot safer. Judging from his behavior there was no doubt that Fletcher was comfortable with Priscilla. He could be in—

Stop. With firm pressure of her fingers, she smoothed the creases of the frown from her forehead. Knowing all the conjecture was only feeding her insecurity, she resolved to think positively. Fletcher cared. Why else would he ask her to come all this way when geologists were a dime a dozen in Corpus? The reason had to be personal. She slapped at a tufted clump of grass. That's all there was to it.

Weary from the useless musing, Casey closed her eyes and gave herself up to drowsiness that seemed to go hand in hand with the heat. It seemed no time at all before the distant rumbling of the one-ton opened her eyes again. She stood, shaking off her lethargy and, with a yawn, greeted the men with a half-hearted wave.

Looking around the charming restaurant with its candlelit tables and plush decor, Casey patted the corners of her lips with a napkin. The food had been palatable, she supposed, not really recalling its taste. At first she had felt excitement at treating herself to dinner in Corpus. She had become restless waiting for Fletcher at the ranch. Even in Mack's company the hours after work seemed to drag by.

Now, as she sat in the elegant dining room of a Corpus hotel and glanced at the couples leaning over their dinners in intimate conversations, Casey felt a loneliness steal over her. Staring at the white tablecloth, she sipped her coffee and wondered if any of the other patrons felt as much at loose ends as she did. She had adjusted to most facets of single life but somehow never learned to enjoy dining alone in a restaurant. The hope that Fletcher would put an end to all that made her bite her lower lip to check the wide smile that taunted her face. Smiles had come spontaneously all day, each time she thought of Fletcher, his arms holding her close.

"Blasting up the countryside certainly seems to agree with you, Casey." The dry comment of Henry Ames exploded her wistful thoughts.

Caught off guard, her blinking gaze swung upward to meet Henry's assessing brown eyes. Instinctively she lifted her chin against his hard stare. "Hello, Henry." A quick glance over his shoulder brought no sign of Priscilla. Thankful, Casey let out a slow breath and hoped the relief didn't show on her face. Fingering one of the tiny pearls at her earlobes, she smiled, searching for some pleasantry to fill the gap in the conversation—a gap that invariably came after the initial exchange of greetings with Henry. There never seemed to be anything more she wanted to say. "Are you alone?" she asked.

"Yes, as a matter of fact, I am. Priscilla's out of town, so I'm on my own tonight." He ran a chubby hand over his balding head. "How about you?"

"Same here," she said with a nod.

Still Henry stood with no pretense of moving on to another table. Casey sipped her coffee and, while peering over the rim of her cup, watched him adjust the waist of his trousers, straighten the lapels of his jacket, and smooth the flaps of his pockets. She half-feared he might whip out a cloth and shine his shoes if she didn't do something fast. It occurred to Casey that Henry might not relish the idea of dining alone any more than she did. But she couldn't suppress a crooked smile that he would find her company preferable to his own.

"Would you like to join me, Henry? I'm finished eating, but a second cup of coffee sounds nice." Before she could motion to the chair opposite her, Henry's heavyset frame was in it.

131

"Thanks, but I can't stay long. Just grabbing a quick bite before going home. Long day, you know."

"Of course," she said, accepting with a measure of grace his I-guess-I-can-spare-you-a-few-minutes tone.

When Henry had ordered his dinner and she sat sipping more hot coffee, Casey wasn't at all surprised that the conversation focused on oil. That, with the possible exception of Priscilla, seemed to be his favorite subject. Throughout his meal she tried to show interest in his enthusiastic monologue, if only because he so obviously appreciated her attention. She also sensed that although he might be a little in awe of her as a geologist, a bona fide oil strike was the only thing that would really convince him of her ability.

Surprised when he sought her opinion of the projected life span of Middle East oil deposits, Casey was nonetheless pleased that he had asked—even if he did take strident issue with her response.

"By the way," he said, crossing his arms on the table, "I was looking over the blasting schedule for the next week. I noticed SR-Four isn't listed. Has Fletcher mentioned anything about that section?"

"Not that I recall," she said absently. "Is there a problem?"

"I don't know. You see, Fletcher and Mack don't own that land anymore, and I can only assume they're trying to buy it back." Henry hesitated a moment, then let out an impatient sigh. "I was hoping the sale would be finalized by now so that we could go ahead with the blasting. Personally, I think the Santa Rosa division has better possibilities than any other part of the ranch."

Casey drew her brows together in a frown. Santa Rosa. Section Four. The realization that Henry was referring to her land oozed over her. She opened her mouth, ready to blurt out the information, but—almost instinctively—

closed it again. She hadn't been told of any plans to test that spot. "Does Fletcher believe SR-Four has—possibilities?"

Henry's wide shoulders lifted in a shrug. "He never speculates about things like that. Not to me, anyway. I can't imagine why he would let a valuable piece of property like that get away from him in the first place." Henry snorted his disapproval. "I'll bet Fletcher Robbins has spent many a sleepless night trying to figure out how to get it back—now that we're looking for oil."

"Oh, I doubt that, Henry." She knew her denial was more for her own defense than Fletcher's. A faint fear that she was at a loss to explain formed a tightness in her chest. Her land had been targeted for cattle use. Fletcher had told her that himself. He had certainly never mentioned that he planned to test that area for oil, although she supposed it would be none of her business, once the papers were signed. But she hadn't signed anything yet and she felt a little cheated. "There must be other divisions that look just as promising for oil deposits," she said. "For instance, the Nueces."

"Maybe." Henry dismissed her comment with a wave of his hand. "It really doesn't matter. Fletcher has assured me that there'll be no problem with SR-Four or any other section. It's all in my contractual agreement with him. From the very beginning he promised my company drilling access to every part of the ranch, including Santa Rosa."

"How could he make such a promise, Henry? I mean— if he doesn't own the land?"

Henry smiled this time. "I've asked that question myself and been told—politely, of course—to mind my own business. But it's obvious from things Fletcher has said that he has personal connections with the owner. He's an astute businessman. He'll get the land back. He'll do whatever he has to do to live up to his end of the bargain."

Whatever he has to do. Did that include wining, dining, and bedding the prospective seller, if necessary? Her jaw tightened to stop the sneer, threatening to curl her lips. Henry went on talking, but she heard none of his words. A rapid pulse pounded in her ears as she fastened her gaze on the carpet and tried to assimilate the information.

In the agreement from the very beginning . . . personal connections with the owner. Fletcher must have planned to recover the land long before she made him an offer. She had just happened to spring the idea on him before he was ready to broach the subject. Before she was sufficiently buttered up. That was the reason he had asked her to come. After all, no geologist in Corpus had what he *really* wanted. That day at Susan's—and several times since—he had refused her offer to sell only a few acres. He had demanded all or nothing—because that's what he had to do. And there's nothing like gentle, persuasive lovemaking to bring a recalcitrant ex-wife around. That hurt more than anything she had considered thus far. She didn't want to believe that Fletcher would do such a thing. Didn't he know she would gladly have given him the land had he only asked?

Her hands clenched into fists beneath the table. Cattle indeed. Fletcher had no intention of using the land for grazing. Well, he could have the land and the oil and be damned. Her commitment to Susan and John gave her no choice in the matter.

Still, she knew there was something else—some question that nagged her and wouldn't be driven away, something Henry had said. . . . Massaging the annoying throb at her temple, she glanced at the portly man opposite her. The question snapped into place. There was one thing more she had to know, and she steeled herself for the answer.

"Henry, you said Priscilla's out of town. Do you know when she and Fletcher will be back from San Antonio?"

"Late this evening probably. Why? Is it important?"

She smiled a bitter, painful smile and shook her head. "No. It isn't important at all."

Without knowing quite how she did so, Casey made her excuses, paid the check, and found herself out in the hotel parking area. As she drove toward the ranch the many thoughts that raced through her mind all condensed into one harrowing conclusion.

She didn't know Fletcher at all anymore. The knowledge shook the very foundation of her existence, frightened her. The realization of just how much she had always depended on his unshakable support, his unwavering faith, even when he wasn't there, sent a jolt of regret through her. The supports were gone now, replaced by . . . what? Greed? Resentment? One thing was certain: She couldn't trust him.

One night of love. That's all it was, and she had tried to turn it into something lasting. To him it must have been the fulfillment of a simple physical need.

Regret dissolved to vengeance as Casey searched for alternatives to selling the land. By the time she parked in the circular drive and switched off the lights of the Scout, no solution had presented itself. With resignation she made her way upstairs to her room and undressed in the darkness. As she slipped beneath the cool covers of the four-poster the vivid, aching memory of Fletcher's arms around her permeated her thoughts. Turning her face to the pillow, she bitterly shoved the image from her mind. Her sleep was restless, fitful, and brought no escape.

Even in her dreams she knew Fletcher's kiss and couldn't deny him. The gentle pressure on her lips compelled her to taste him, to experience the heady teasing of masculine fingers moving across her breasts. Seeking a firmer commitment from his mouth, she found him elusive, taunting her cheeks, her eyes with butterfly kisses. *Oh, God, don't tease me, Fletcher.* But he moved away. Her frustration peaked at the sound of his low, almost sardonic chuckle. Reality groped its way through the haze of her sleep. Her eyes fluttered open to the shadowy silhouette that was Fletcher.

A sudden flood of light from the bedside table made her turn away, cringing from the intrusion. She rubbed her eyes and summoned the strength to face him. "How was San Antonio?" she managed, forcing the sleep from her voice.

"It's still there," he said casually. Her wall of defense almost toppled when she turned back to his deceptively affectionate smile. "I made a deal to buy a herd of Black Angus, but frankly, an all-day discussion of four-legged creatures didn't much appeal to me today."

She knew he was going to kiss her. In panic at her own temptation to let him, she moved to the other side of the bed. Adjusting her gown to cover her breasts, she sat against a propped pillow. "I can't imagine that being much fun for Priscilla. I hope you made it up to her."

"I think she enjoyed the party to celebrate the deal well enough. In fact, she didn't want to leave." He sat on the bed and took her hand. "*I* had good reason to get home tonight, though."

He was good, Casey thought coolly. So good that with a little more— She gripped her faltering conviction. Pulling her hand from the coaxing pressure of his, she made a pretense of raking the mass of tangled hair away from her face. The motion only seemed to encourage him. He moved closer and began stroking the sensitive skin on the inside of her wrist. God, did he think she was playing the shy lover, waiting for some declaration, some sign of his caring? Again, she blocked his caress to fluff the pillow behind her.

"How did you feel this morning?" he asked.

"Fine. How about you?" Her voice was as full of nonchalance as she could make it.

He paused for a moment as if searching her eyes before he continued. "Any regrets?"

"Why, no," she said with a shrug. "Should I have?"

"Well . . . we didn't have much of a chance to talk."

Lucky for you, she thought bitterly, then forced a sultry smile. "There didn't seem to be any need for that."

"Maybe. I'd like to know your feelings, though."

She surprised herself with a lilting laugh. "Why so serious, Fletcher? It was a very enjoyable interlude for both of us. I think we should leave it at that."

"Leave it?" He looked stunned.

For a moment she thought she would lash out at him—slap the wary confusion from his face. But she didn't. The pain cut too deep, surpassing anger. To get through it—that was all she could hope for tonight. "We just followed our natural instincts, Fletcher. One night for old time's sake." Her courage faltered as the sparks of anger ignited in his eyes and blood colored his face. "I hope you're not making too much of it."

"Is that all it was to you?"

"Well, I have to admit that you certainly swept me off my feet," she said nervously, then nudged her contempt forward. "But then I have to remember that you always were good in bed."

"I see." With a sneer he rose and turned away, his hands clenched into fists. "Do you just follow your *natural instincts* whenever the feeling hits you?" He shook his head and swore under his breath. "When did you become such a callous, coldhearted woman, Casey?"

She trembled at the sting of his words. An almost overpowering urge to tell him the truth rushed forth like a tidal wave inside her. But raw pride kept her from confessing her love. "I've learned to face reality, Fletcher. I take my pleasures where I find them. One night with you doesn't mean I'm ready for reconciliation." She winced inside, unable to believe she was saying the words. "I thought you'd feel the same way."

"Right now, I feel like flogging you!"

She felt the steel grip of his hands on her shoulders as he lifted her from the bed to stand before him. She shuddered at the chill in his eyes. Taking a deep breath, she forced calm to her voice. "Let go, Fletcher. I'm tired—so tired."

The muscles in his jaw clenched. His fingers dug into her flesh. For a long, silent moment he stared at her quivering lips before he finally released her and turned away. "What happened to us, Casey?"

Her heart wrenched at the hurt in his voice as tears for herself and for him sprang to her eyes. "I don't know," she said quietly. "But it's over."

Casey walked mechanically to the bathroom and closed the door behind her. Leaning against it, she let the tears flow. The painful finality of it all racked her body and left her weak with despair.

"It isn't over, Casey." His voice echoed through the door. "It will *never* be over." The click of the bedroom door as it closed left her to ponder the meaning of his words.

It *was* over. It had never even begun. With a conscious effort she forced her trembling to subside and her breathing to some semblance of normalcy. She would begin the slow healing process again. This time she would purge her heart of Fletcher permanently and she would do it in his presence. Never again would she leave with any regrets or recriminations over Fletcher Robbins. Never again!

CHAPTER EIGHT

"Sit down and pass the salt, Casey." Mack's voice came rumbling across the table as he attacked his toast with butter and knife. "I don't know why we have to have these early phone calls to interrupt a man's breakfast."

"You're certainly a grizzly bear this morning," she said, obeying his grumpy command. She tried not to smile at the fact that *her* breakfast was the one that was interrupted. "Didn't you sleep well last night?"

"I did all right. How about you?" Mack's raised eyebrow only emphasized his penetrating gaze.

"If you're asking how I slept, the answer is fine," she replied, aware that Fletcher was probably listening intently behind his newspaper at the head of the table.

"Well, I missed you at dinner," Mack continued, stabbing a piece of ham.

"I had a wonderful dinner in Corpus at that new hotel, then I came back here. Have you been there, Mack? It's really charming."

"No." Mack lowered his gaze to his plate. "See anybody we know?"

"Steve Howard." Casey consciously omitted the name

140

of Henry Ames. She was still too upset to stand up to the questions Fletcher might possibly come up with. And she had in fact exchanged a brief hello with Steve Howard, who had been entering the restaurant with a date just as she had been running out. She flinched, the sudden rattle of newspaper startling her.

"Howard? That women's doctor?" Mack chuckled, then took a gulp of coffee. "I'll bet you left that wimp choking on your heel dust, didn't you."

"No, Mack, I didn't. And I don't think that's a very polite description of Steve." Casey smoothed her napkin a little tighter across her lap. "As a matter of fact, I'm having dinner with him next Friday. He's calling later this week to let me know where to meet him."

"What? Why would you want to waste your time with that namby-pamby?" Mack nodded vigorously despite her warning glance. "I'm sorry, Casey, but I call 'em as I see 'em, and that guy—"

"Mack." Fletcher folded the paper and set it beside his plate. "This is really none of our business. What Casey does with her free time is her concern."

Now, that's the Fletcher I know, she thought, concentrating on her eggs Benedict. Whether it was understanding or indifference, she didn't know, but his attitude was familiar at least.

"Mack, what are your plans for the day?" Casey asked in an attempt to erase the moping expression from the older man's face.

"Oh, I don't know." Mack tossed his napkin onto the table. "Maybe I'll ride some."

"Great. That's what I'm going to do. Come with me, Mack," she suggested with a coaxing smile. "I could pack a picnic lunch, and we could ride all day. I'd like to take a look at my land."

"I don't think so." Mack frowned. "You always pack

141

those awful tuna sandwiches. I never said anything before, Casey, but tuna is just not my idea of a man's food."

Rolling her gaze to the ceiling, Casey shook her head and deepened her voice. "Is roast beef macho enough for you, Mack?"

"Better." He shrugged. "But now that I think about it, I'd rather get in my truck and drive to the beach. I always find that relaxing when I've got things on my mind." Mack pushed back his chair and rose. "Fletcher, you go riding with her."

Casey looked to Fletcher for his excuses and caught the annoyance in his eyes.

"You haven't been to the beach in twenty years," Fletcher pointed out casually. "But you go ahead, Mack. And while you're there you might want to work on your subtlety."

Mack strolled to the dining room door, then turned back with a mischievous grin. "Subtlety never got me anywhere, Son. If I'd used that tactic with your mother, Casey might be staring at an empty chair right now."

Casey quickly shifted her gaze from Fletcher to her plate and tried to turn back the warm tide of color that crept to her face. Mack had to be the most exasperating man, she thought, but she couldn't stop the smile that teased the corners of her lips. She brought a hand to her mouth to hide her amusement as she listened to the click of Mack's boots in the hall, then the slam of the front door.

"Well, I guess you'll have to settle for me." It was almost a challenge as Fletcher rose, scratching the back of his head.

"You don't have to come with me. You're not dressed for riding." She avoided the dark brown slacks that stretched across his powerful hips and thighs.

"It'll only take a minute to change. If you insist on seeing the land, it's best if someone goes with you." He walked to the door and turned back, just as Mack had done. "Besides," he added dryly, "you know how *I* feel about tuna."

She wrinkled her nose and frowned, then stiffened at the searching look in his eyes. "All right." Casey lowered her gaze and pushed herself away from the table. "I'll make the lunch and meet you at the stables."

"Good. See you in a few minutes."

Casey walked to the kitchen and sighed as she tried to hold both a twinge of fear and tingling pleasure at bay. A whole day with Fletcher, she thought, absently scanning the contents of the refrigerator. Indifference was the only way to play his game without getting hurt. She would have to keep a tight rein on her emotions, especially her anger. Fletcher could spot that and turn it into desire so fast. Yes, she would steamroller her way through the day and not allow him to play with her feelings. That was too risky.

When the sandwiches were made Casey divided the picnic into two leather satchels and slung the straps to her shoulders. Snatching her hat, she stepped outside for a deep breath of fresh morning air before walking alongside the rambling split-rail fence toward the stables.

Morning glories entwined the rough-hewn planks and opened their dew-kissed petals to embrace the sun's warmth. Honey bees buzzed from flower to flower to drink the sweet nectar, as if sensing that soon the hot midday sun would deny them precious access until evening, when the petals would unfold invitingly again.

Casey leaned against a post and rested a booted foot on one of the rails. As she looked beyond to a lush green pasture, a covey of ducks left their camouflage in the tall grass and took to the air with soaring grace.

That's what I should do too, Casey thought, watching until the birds became tiny brown dots on the horizon. She knew she couldn't leave yet, though. Not until she had fulfilled her promise to rid herself of her tormenting love for Fletcher.

As he emerged from the barn Casey watched him lead a striking albino mare and the gray stallion from the paddock.

"He's beautiful, Fletcher." Closer inspection revealed a white star just below the horse's forelock. "What's his name?"

"Cinder," Fletcher replied, tightening the cinch below the horse's belly. "We bought him last year. I saddled Marengo for you. She's spirited at times, so you have to watch her."

"Oh, I think we'll get along just fine." Casey rubbed Marengo's forehead, then tossed one of the satchels to Fletcher.

"What's this?" he asked, looping the strap around his saddle horn.

"Picnic supplies—plates, cups, you know. I've got the food in here." She patted the leather bag that now hung from Marengo's saddle.

"Hmmm. Let's hope we don't get separated. I'd hate to starve in the middle of the Wild Horse Desert."

"The ranch is hardly a desert anymore, Fletcher. Not since your family discovered the artesian wells and built dams." She eyed the sheathed Winchester that Fletcher was never without when he rode the range. He had even insisted that she carry a lightweight gun on her solitary outings. "Do you really need that rifle these days?"

"Rarely," he replied, gathering Cinder's reins. "But there are still coyotes and bobcats around, Casey. Don't forget that when you go riding alone. A gun comes in handy to signal trouble, too."

She nodded noncommittally and mounted Marengo. At the cluck of Casey's tongue the mare started across the field at an easy, natural gait. Although Cinder matched

144

the pace, Casey sensed the stallion's restlessness. She pushed her hat firmly to her head and urged Marengo to a brisk canter that soon evolved into a full gallop.

It felt good to ride with Fletcher again, Casey thought as she admired his gray stallion's mane outstretched in the wind. The fast clip lasted only a few minutes, though, when Fletcher's signal slowed the horses to a lope. He lifted his Stetson to rake his fingers through his blond hair before replacing the hat again.

"Casey, I'm surprised you care enough to see your land before you sign it over to me."

She stiffened inwardly. "When will that be, Fletcher?" She couldn't fathom the expression in his eyes, but at least there was no hint of smug triumph.

"It's up to you," he replied. "My attorney can draw up the sale any time you say. There's really no sense in waiting if you need the money soon."

"I suppose not." She sighed. "I am curious to know what I'm giving up. Where is the property anyway?"

"About a mile from here." He turned Cinder in an easterly direction and motioned Casey to ride beside him.

"Fletcher, are you still planning to use it for cattle?" she asked, uncertain of her resolution to remain indifferent.

"I don't know, Casey. Parts of it would make good grazing for cattle. It has water that has to be pumped, but the windmills take care of that. The lowlands would be good for truck crops. I tried to see that you got a cross section."

And now you want it all back. She felt a bitter ache rise within her and tried to stop its spreading. He'd made no mention of the oil. But that must be the real reason he wanted the land. She looked away toward a group of black-bellied tree ducks, perched on the branches of a hackberry. It was clear Fletcher wasn't going to volunteer any information. Whatever she wanted to know she would have to extract from him. "Henry seems eager to have SR-Four tested. Would you like me to add it to the blasting schedule? I could work it in before we decide on a site."

"There's plenty of time for that later, Casey. If the first well comes in, the entire ranch will be subject to testing. I'm aware that Henry thinks that piece of ground is saturated with crude."

She focused her eyes on the almost-healed gash that only intensified the ruggedness of his face. "And you, Fletcher. What do you think?"

His confident gaze slid to hers. "I think it has damn good possibilities. Why?"

"Never mind. It doesn't matter." She tapped Marengo's flanks, urging the mare to a trot.

So, it was true, she thought. Not only did Fletcher want all his land consolidated again, but he held out hope for oil, too. Why hadn't he just written her instead of bringing her here on a professional pretense? Instead of stirring the embers of desire and love into a consuming flame again?

They rode in silence until the horses carried them to a ridge that overlooked a wide expanse of prairie grass. Casey watched as cowpunchers expertly moved a Charolais herd to the next grazing pasture. One of the men drove the huge white lead steer out in front as other cowboys on sturdy cutting horses rounded up strays and coaxed the whining, bellowing cattle forward.

"That fence just ahead marks the boundary of your property," Fletcher said absently.

Casey tried to hide her eagerness to set foot on her domain and see all that it offered, but her breathing quickened in spite of her efforts. Even Marengo seemed restless and began to dance and chafe at the bit before Casey snapped the reins and guided the horse in a zigzag path down the gentle slope. On flatland again, Casey's ability as an accomplished horsewoman blended with Marengo's surefootedness and, together, they shot across the pasture at breakneck speed.

When the fence loomed before them, Marengo cleared the rough plank with ease, and Casey felt the exhilaration of jumping again. The horse's hooves clapped the dry dirt at a slower pace until Casey pulled in the reins and turned to see Fletcher, staring from the ridge where she had left him. She waved him forward with an encouraging smile. He traced her path down the ridge through the tall grass. Matching her speed, he and Cinder sailed neatly over the fence, then slowed to join her.

No words were spoken, and yet Casey felt a silent message pass between her and Fletcher. A message of companionship. Together they burst into laughter, and for a moment she experienced that same camaraderie, that same love of so long ago. The laughter died, though, and the pain of reality came over her again.

She turned away and rode toward a row of date palms in the distance. She knew the trees weren't native to the land. They were an experiment of the first Mrs. Robbins. An experiment that failed; for not more than a few of the palms had ever taken hold in the dry climate of the Wild Horse Desert. Still, Casey held admiration for the woman who set the standard for all the succeeding Robbins wives. A standard that she, Casey, hadn't quite reached during her tenure as mistress of the Circle R. Offhand she couldn't think of one contribution she'd made toward the betterment of the ranch.

Perhaps if she could guide Fletcher to the oil, that would be her redemption, even if she wasn't mistress anymore. Maybe that's what Fletcher had in mind. Another chance to— *No*, she told herself firmly. *Don't let your mind play tricks, Casey. You had your chance.*

When they moved on to the lowlands, she imagined a

huge, healthy cotton field spread before her, its white bolls as big as her fists. In the background of her mind a two-story house with a red clay roof, just like Fletcher's hacienda, stood in the midst of ebony trees. Her vision seemed to crystalize and shatter to fall at her feet.

She sighed, knowing that even if she wasn't selling the land, she could never live alone on the property so close to Fletcher. She could never bring an outsider here, either, and she wasn't the type to live a cloistered life, pining for a man she couldn't have.

Fletcher dismounted near a creek that had been dammed to catch and hold precious rainwater. He led Cinder to the water as Casey slid from Marengo's back and followed his lead. She stretched the muscles in her arms and shoulders, now uncomfortably hot from the glaring rays of the sun directly overhead.

"This looks like a nice spot for a picnic." He smiled and waited for her response.

"Yes, it's cool here with trees for shade." Casey removed her hat and searched one of the leather satchels for the checkered tablecloth she had packed, then spread it on the carpet of grass.

As Casey unpacked the other supplies Fletcher skipped rocks across the creek, and soon Casey found herself mentally counting the number of times each pebble skimmed the water before sinking to the bottom. She decided to try it herself. Abandoning the lunch for a moment, she selected a small stone from the bank and poised her arm as Fletcher had done. Her misguided throw promptly sent the rock to the bottom with a discouraging plop.

She wrinkled her nose as Fletcher chuckled and placed another pebble in her hand.

"The flat ones work better. This time, give it a little snap with your wrist," he said, flexing that part of her hand.

She tried to ignore the electricity of his touch but that,

148

coupled with the magnetic appeal of his blue-gray eyes, set her defenses on guard and made her pull her hand, however reluctantly, from his. Bringing her elbow shoulder high, she flung the pebble with a snap of her wrist. Before she could count more than two skips she felt Fletcher's hand on her shoulder. Closing her eyes, Casey willed her mind to deny his caressing congratulations.

"Well, enough of that. I'm hungry," she said in the lightest tone she could manage.

Not risking another glance at him, she turned and walked back to finish the preparations for lunch. When Fletcher joined her, sitting cross-legged on the grass, he poured red wine for two and offered a glass to her. They ate their lunch in relative silence, mingled with casual conversation about the land and the oil business. Casey sensed his efforts to ease her tension, and once or twice felt her resolve slip at his natural charm and wit. Each time, though, she redoubled her determination to keep her distance—emotionally, at least.

"You know, I've been thinking," he said, setting his wine aside. "This is the first time we've ever worked together on a business project."

"Yes, it's you, me, Priscilla, and Henry," she retorted in an attempt to drive a psychological wedge between them. "Where is Priscilla, anyway? I thought you might want to spend a well-earned day off with her."

"She's staying with friends in San Antonio for a few days. I believe she said she needed time to think." Fletcher's tone was dry, as if he found the excuse trite.

"Oh? Trouble in paradise?" Immediately she regretted the question and hoped he would ignore her cattiness.

"I really couldn't say." He sipped his wine, then smiled. "It would seem that women find 'time to think' a convenient excuse to run away from problems."

She stiffened at his insinuation. "Sometimes, when

problems are insolvable, getting away seems the only recourse."

He shrugged. "Don't you think it's important to discover what the *real* problems are before trying to escape them?" He turned a thoughtful gaze toward the creek.

Casey sensed that he didn't really need a response from her. She wouldn't have known how to answer his question, anyway. But now she realized the reason he had wanted to come riding. He was feeling at loose ends without Priscilla, and *anyone's* company would have served the same purpose in Priscilla's absence.

After a moment's hesitation he turned back to her. "You know, there was a time when I couldn't imagine being in love with the same woman forever. Then I met you and—well, when I found myself approaching that very predicament, it wasn't an easy adjustment." He shook his head and cast her a cynical smile that made her pulse throb. Then his smile turned to a searching frown. "I knew that I loved you, but the fear that it wouldn't last always lurked in the back of my mind. Even with all that, I was still shocked when all my fears came true. A self-fulfilling prophecy, perhaps?"

"Don't talk like that, Fletcher." Her voice was pleading as she rose and walked to the clear water.

What was he trying to do? she wondered. Excuse his part in the marriage and divorce, so that the blame would rest completely with her? She heard his whisper at her ear as his hands rested on her shoulders.

"I'm not offering excuses for my shortcomings, Casey," he said, as if reading her thoughts. "Only an explanation. I suppose I never let you see how caught up I was in our marriage—just in case it all came crashing down around me."

Casey could only think how much she wanted to believe him. How much she wanted another chance. When he turned her to him and kissed her trembling lips, the doubts became cloudy and distant. God, she hated his ability to do that to her. Gradually his firm mouth went soft against hers, asking, coaxing, and ultimately demanding a response. She wrenched her lips from his and glared up at him, hoping she wouldn't have to speak—knowing she couldn't have done so.

There was unrelenting challenge in narrowed eyes. His hand traveled slowly up and down her arms. And though his touch filled her with an ache that was almost too much to bear, she found she needed his support for the simple act of remaining on her feet. Neither could she ignore the rapid rise and fall of her breasts, brushing the hardness of his chest with each gulp of air she took.

It was the deepening crease at the corner of his mouth that first told her he was fully aware of her desperation. Then the infuriating tilted smile that followed made her insides twist with yearning. He made no move toward her but waited this time for her to come to him. And she did, hating herself all the way for being so weak, for giving in to the devastation of his passive attack. When his lips took hers in a slow, agonizing assault, a tiny denial—however cramped for space—remained in her mind.

It's only this place, she told herself. It was his intimate sharing of feelings that made her want him so much. She shouldn't let her emotions foreshadow good judgment. But her arms refused to bow to any judgment. They slipped upward around his neck and pulled him closer. She drew a faltering breath when his lips branded a trail from the soft flesh below her ear to the aching hollow between her breasts. Hot shivers raced through her veins as he pushed the gauze fabric of her blouse aside and let his tongue flick over the sensitive curves. Hands that seemed content with circular caresses of her waist and ribs suddenly crushed her against him.

151

She had no strength to hold her head, and let it fall back with a gasp at the exquisite wandering of his lips. She filled her hands with hard thighs, sinewy hips.

The empty years without him seemed to ebb and flow from the center of her thoughts to the far corners of her mind and back again. There was no eye of the hurricane, where she could find shelter, peace from this man. *Damn him. Damn him,* she moaned to herself. He knew her too well. He knew how his hands could delight every nerve. No matter how she chose to deny it—by a lift of her chin or a hateful glare—he knew her like no other man ever could.

But when his lips came home to hers with such tender, raw appeal, she could only clutch his shoulders and hold him to her. His warm, sensuous tongue gliding over her mouth redoubled the need cascading through her. Would it always be this way? Please, let it . . . always.

She let her hands rove his muscular back, then slid shaking fingers inside his shirt to explore the silken tangle of hair on his chest. Her thumb rested at the sensitive chord of his neck while the pounding of her heart matched the rhythm of his own. He cupped her chin and tilted her head back as his fiery gaze captured her emerald eyes.

"You belong here, Casey." His voice was a husky whisper. "You and this land share a reckless beauty—an untamed spirit. Soon I'll have the land again, but I won't stop until I have you, too."

She caught her breath as the meaning of his words settled over her. The mention of her land brought all the doubts rushing back to her mind, leaving no room for the wanton passion that had gripped her only moments ago. She pushed away from his grasp, her body trembling with the realization that he had come so close to his goal. He must have seen the storm in her eyes, for he made no attempt to hold on to her.

"No, Fletcher." Again she was forced to use bravado when courage failed her. "I won't be cornered."

"And I won't be denied." He lifted one eyebrow as though to emphasize his determination.

His penetrating gaze remained on her, increasing her already-rapid pulse until she thought she might scream if he didn't stop staring. Tossing her raven hair, she walked away and began stuffing the picnic supplies into the satchels.

"Fletcher, I agreed to help you find oil. I've agreed to sell you the land. Don't ask for anything more than that. I won't play your stupid games!" She knew she was shouting but couldn't stop herself, until Fletcher gripped her shoulders and turned her to him, holding her close.

"Be quiet, Casey," he whispered in a soothing voice. "I won't push you anymore—not now, anyway." He lifted her chin and smiled. "But if you think that all we've shared is business, then one of us is a fool."

"Good God!" She flung his arm away. "Don't you ever stop?" Casey grabbed Marengo's reins and lifted herself to the horse's back. "You know, Fletcher, sometimes I come very close to hating you."

"And how do you feel the rest of the time?"

"Drained!" she snapped.

He shook his head and sighed. "If hating me takes that much energy, you're trying too hard."

She bestowed an icy glare, then urged Marengo into a gallop.

Before she had gone more than two or three miles, her anger had changed to exasperation and confusion. Distrust still loomed in her mind, but she knew she had lied to him. He was so much a part of her that hating him would be like hating herself. Although she had experienced self-hate a few times lately, she had to admit the feeling had passed as quickly as it had come.

Casey looked behind her to see Fletcher and Cinder, tracing her trail at a placid lope. She knew he must have ridden hard and fast to catch up so quickly, apparently slowing his pace when he spotted her. Motioning for him to join her, she shook her head and smiled when Fletcher whistled, then slapped Cinder's flank with his hat and galloped to her side.

"I'm glad to know you still want my company," he said, replacing his hat.

"It isn't that, Fletcher," she lied again. "I just want you where I can keep an eye on you. That's all. Now, if you'll be so good as to race me home, I'll beat the pants off you."

His mouth twisted into a devilish grin. "Now, that's an angle I hadn't thought of, but—"

She left his words hanging in the air as she held on to her hat and sped across the prairie grass. Skirting a herd of Santa Gertrudis, she laughed at the surprised faces of the cowboys as she dashed by them, the wind lifting her hair and making her spirits soar.

By the time Casey reached the ridge Fletcher was hot on her heels. Cinder and Marengo were neck and neck on the home stretch, but Casey knew she still had a chance to win. From the corner of her eye she saw Fletcher's strong, sure hands guiding Cinder as though man and horse were of one accord. With a last burst of effort she urged Marengo on and gradually took over the lead. When the stable loomed before her, Casey checked the mare's speed and jumped to the ground.

Tossing the reins to a waiting ranch hand, she ran to the house and flung open the screen door, then heard it slam behind her. Before she was halfway up the stairs she heard the slam again, and shivers of excitement rippled through her as she raced down the hall and into the bedroom. With a victory smile she sprawled onto the bed and gasped for air. The smile froze on her face when she saw Fletcher's curious stare as he leaned against the doorframe. Humiliation seized her when she realized what she had done. It had been a tradition during their marriage to end all horse races in Fletcher's arms—in this room, which they had shared. She leaped from his bed as though it were a hot branding iron.

"So you remembered the rules of the game." Fletcher tossed his hat onto the bed and walked toward her.

She brushed past him, but stopped at the sound of his voice.

"Don't be ashamed of your memories or your feelings, Casey. We had something special, once."

She closed her eyes to the whisper in his voice. "Maybe, but I intend to get on with the future."

"Can you forget the love?"

"It's no good without trust," she answered, too tired to say any more.

"If you're thinking of Steve—"

"Steve?" Her hands clenched into fists as she held her rage in check. Turning to him, she bit her lip to stop its trembling. "I'm going to say this once, then don't ever mention it again. I never had an affair with Steve or anyone else."

"I know that now, but why did you—"

"Leave?" She supplied the word for him. "Because you didn't trust me, Fletcher. You didn't believe me and you didn't care. There was nothing to hold on to." She turned on her heels and walked in a daze to her room.

CHAPTER NINE

"Dr. Howard called to say he would be a few minutes late," the young hostess with copper curls explained with an apologetic smile. "An emergency, I believe. Shall I show you to your table?"

"Please." Casey nodded and followed the girl to the table Steve had reserved.

Only a few people dressed in casual wear occupied the restaurant, and Casey was grateful for a few moments to reacquaint herself with the place before Steve's arrival. She took a seat and surveyed the dimly lit surroundings of the Black Diamond Oyster Bar. The sea motif had changed very little since she had dined there with Fletcher in years gone by. Intricately designed seashells still dotted the huge seines that draped the sea-green walls, and the large aquarium filled with sponges and multicolored fish remained the focal point of the decor. Even with candle-light and soft music the oyster bar couldn't be considered elegant, but it could be as intimate as its patrons cared to make it.

Fingering one of the tiny pearls at her earlobe, Casey sighed, remembering that Fletcher had chosen to make it deliciously intimate. But tonight was different. Tonight she would dine with an old friend and talk over old times. As she adjusted the tortoiseshell combs that held her ebony hair away from her face, she hoped the mood would be pleasant and casual and that she would be able to shake off her preoccupation with Susan's phone call earlier in the day. Indecision clouded her mind again as she remembered her sister's reason for calling.

John had found another investor for the fishing boat. Just like that, someone had stepped forward to put up the money. There was no need to sell the land now.

She should be relieved, happy, she told herself, sipping the red wine Steve had ordered to be served in his absence. At least she would have the satisfaction of beating Fletcher at his own game. But the victory would be small consolation for the hurt she had sustained at his hands. What real good would come from denying him the land, anyway? she wondered. It would only keep her tied to the ranch and memories and Fletcher.

Casey raised slender fingers to the sleeve of her mint-green blouse and traced the diamond-shaped pattern of its satiny smooth material. Soon the fate of the land would have to be decided, she supposed. But not tonight. She would enjoy herself and not allow thoughts of Fletcher to spoil the evening.

As Steve entered the restaurant Casey peered over the rim of her glass and smiled. His brown suit, brown tie, brown shirt, and thinning brown hair made her wonder wryly if he might also be wearing brown underwear. Then an uncomfortable feeling wiped the smile from her face as her gaze slid past Steve to see Fletcher, watching her with a curious expression. Priscilla clung to his arm, and Casey mentally commanded her heart to stop its vigorous pounding as the three walked toward her.

One glance at the light-blue tailored suit that hugged

Fletcher's shoulders and thighs made Casey lower her gaze and reach for a glass of water. Questions raced through her mind. Why had he come here? How had he known where she would be? She had seen him so little the past few days that she thought he might have forgotten her dinner plans with Steve.

Greetings sailed past her, and she went through the motions in a daze. Only when Steve sat beside her and Fletcher and Priscilla occupied the chairs across the table did Casey absorb Steve's explanation of meeting them outside in the parking lot.

"Naturally, I asked them to join us," Steve continued. "I was sure you wouldn't mind."

"Absolutely not." Aware that it could only be Fletcher's knee that pressed against her thigh beneath the table, Casey lifted her chin and glared into his blue-gray eyes before moving away from his touch. Then she turned to Priscilla, who looked as irritated as she, herself, felt. "When did you return from San Antonio, Priscilla?"

"Yesterday." Priscilla patted her elegantly coiffed chignon and smiled. "Fletcher met me at the airport, and we had a quiet dinner at our favorite restaurant."

"How nice for you." Casey lowered her gaze and tried desperately to hide her anger. Had Fletcher come to spy so that he could see for himself just what kind of relationship she really had with Steve? Or was he playing the sympathetic ex-husband, wanting to know that she was settled in another relationship before he married Priscilla? Both explanations were abhorrent to Casey and set her teeth on edge as the waiter arrived with three more glasses and menus.

"Fletcher must be keeping you busy, Casey," Steve said, filling the glasses. "I've been trying to reach you all week, but you never returned my calls. Finally I left a message with Ella this morning to let you know where to meet me tonight. I wasn't even sure you'd show up."

Suspicion filled Casey's thoughts as she turned a sideways glance toward Fletcher. "Who did you talk to the other times, Steve?"

"Mack," Steve replied, surveying the menu.

Casey gripped the laminated plastic tightly in her fingers. Underhanded as Mack's tricks were, she couldn't bring herself to betray him. Had he acted on Fletcher's orders? she wondered.

"I've hardly seen Casey myself the past few days," Fletcher offered smoothly. "Since we decided on a drilling site she's been dividing her time between the well and a geological lab in Corpus." He shrugged an apology. "She's been doing my dirty work."

"Yes, and it looks like I'm not the only one," Casey muttered.

"What did you say?" Steve laid the menu aside and looked up.

"She said she'd like more wine," Fletcher said, filling her half-empty glass.

"Well, I'm ready to order." Steve rested his elbows on the table. "What looks good to you, Casey?"

"I'd like the king crab, I think." She decided to dismiss thoughts of Mack in favor of the succulent dish. "And would you care to share an order of oysters on the half shell?"

Steve made a face at her suggestion. "None for me, thanks. Maybe Fletcher or Priscilla . . ."

"I don't think so." Priscilla spoke as though the thought made her shudder.

That left only Fletcher. Not wanting to appear rude, Casey shot him a questioning stare that she hoped would convey her irritation at his presence.

Fletcher looked up from his menu as though he'd heard

159

none of the conversation. "Casey, did you want something?" he asked flippantly.

Anger seething inside her, Casey took a deep breath and exhaled. "The oysters. Would you like to share an order?"

"So nice of you to ask." Fletcher's smile was mocking. "I'd love to."

Relief spread over Casey when the waiter returned and took Fletcher's attention away from her. As he and Steve gave the orders she used the precious time to collect herself and push the fear of an impending storm to the back of her mind. Surely she could spend an evening in Fletcher's company with a minimum of discomfort. But Fletcher was different tonight. The look in his eyes was almost one of quiet desperation. Had something happened with Priscilla? she wondered, glancing at the blue-eyed woman across the table. No, Priscilla seemed calm enough.

"Casey, I hope you'll have time to play a few rounds of golf with me while you're here," Steve said, his hand resting on her shoulder.

Casey tried to relax the muscles beneath his touch, but Fletcher's gaze, fixed on Steve's hand, made it almost impossible. "I don't know. I'll be quite busy next week, Steve."

"And don't forget that appointment we have with my attorney," Fletcher reminded her, his eyes still fastened on her shoulder.

"We need to talk about that." Casey preferred to discuss the land privately, but now that Fletcher had broached the subject, there seemed no recourse but to tell him. "I'd like to hold off on selling the land. I'm just not ready yet."

Fletcher's tone was cool. "What made you change your mind?"

Casey sighed. "The investment I planned fell through. I won't be needing the cash after all."

"You're not just holding out for a better offer, are you?" he asked.

Casey stiffened with irritation. He would probably get his precious land eventually, but she was in no mood to reassure him now.

"If a better offer comes along, I'll certainly consider it." There. Let him stew over that for a while, she thought with smug satisfaction.

Anger flashed in Fletcher's eyes. "If I had known you were even thinking along those lines, I never would have —" He stopped himself with a sigh of exasperation. "Well, we can discuss this later. Steve, what's been keeping you busy these days?" he asked with amazing cordiality.

"Same old thing," Steve replied. "Delivering babies, mostly."

"Ah, well, that must be rewarding work." Fletcher smiled and sipped his wine.

"Yes, it is." Steve nodded. "Although the hours seem to get longer every day, it's worth it to see loving parents look at new life for the first time."

"Never having had the experience, I'll have to take your word for it." The languid tone in Fletcher's voice made Casey follow his gaze to the center of the restaurant, where a toddler stood, his nose pressed against the glass of the aquarium. The look of warmth in Fletcher's eyes as he watched the small boy sent a pang of regret spiraling through Casey.

"I hope to have children someday," Priscilla interjected dreamily.

"So you've told me many times," Fletcher said with a slight smile, as if humoring a child.

"How about you, Casey?" Priscilla continued.

"Well, I—"

"It's probably better if a woman like Casey doesn't have children," Fletcher interrupted, directing his words to

Priscilla. "You see, her life is so full that a child would only be a burden."

Casey studied the tablecloth in silence and bit back the words of contempt that formed in her mind. What was he trying to do? she wondered. Cut her to the core? It seemed he had come especially to hurt her tonight.

Grateful for the arrival of their dinner, Casey could only pick at the crab, forcing herself to taste it now and then to avoid drawing attention to her state of numbness. She managed to eat two or three oysters dipped in cocktail sauce, but each one deepened her despair a little more, especially when she recalled the breathtaking evenings she had spent here with Fletcher.

Steve's running conversation with Priscilla saved Casey from further contribution, but the questioning, curious glances from Fletcher plagued her so that just the passive act of sitting in her chair took all her will and determination.

"Travel is all right," Priscilla said in answer to some question Casey had missed. "It's nice to visit other places, but I've come to realize how dependent I am on home and traditions and friends who care. I guess I thrive on close relationships. Casey, don't you find it hard to always be tripping off to parts unknown?"

Casey bristled inside at Priscilla's obvious attempt to hold the two women up for comparison. Before she could reply with well-chosen words, Fletcher's harsh chuckle sounded in her ears.

"You must be kidding, Priscilla." The amusement in his voice couldn't hide the contempt in his eyes. "The only reason Casey needs a home at all is to drop off her dirty laundry. And she can do without people, too. Close relationships cramp her style. You're looking at a woman who is totally self-sufficient. Any man who thinks he might be important to her is certainly chasing windmills. Hey, Casey?"

Facing him with outward calm, Casey's mind reeled at his hostile attack. However, she refused to be baited. "You could be right. Perhaps when the right man comes along . . ."

"Yes." Fletcher cocked his head and smiled skeptically. "One with the hide of an armadillo to match yours."

Priscilla smothered a giggle. "I think he's trying to say you're tough-skinned, Casey."

"Thanks for the translation," Casey snapped.

"I don't see anything wrong with that," Steve said in defense. "Fletcher, aren't you the one who always said women have to be as tough as men sometimes?"

"Yes, I suppose I did," Fletcher admitted. Tossing his napkin to the table, he clasped his hands beneath his chin. "But even men have a soft, vulnerable side that makes them human."

"Are you saying now that I'm not human?" Casey asked incredulously.

"Of course not. You've had your sentimental moments, silly as they might seem to some. Take these oysters." Fletcher nodded toward the empty shells on the table. "Casey used to love sharing them with me, but tonight each one caught in her throat. And I can remember a time when she wouldn't have left this restaurant without taking the shells home with—"

"Excuse me." Casey pushed back her chair and rose. "I'd like to see the aquarium."

"Shall I go with you?" Steve offered.

"No. I won't be long." Casey cast him a grateful, though thin smile and walked to the huge tank that held center stage in the restaurant.

As she stood on weak legs and watched the tiny fish swim past she was hardly aware of their striking colors.

163

Fletcher's comments sent her thoughts spinning back to a time when, in this place, she had been more than willing to share oysters with him. She had always insisted that the shells be washed and taken home as souvenirs. He had laughed at the ritual she followed but tolerated her strict adherence to the tradition that began with their first evening here. She could almost hate him now for stripping her of all the traditions she had shared with him.

Then truth oozed into her mind, and Casey found she had only herself to blame. *She* was the one who had left, too immature to face the problems, too young to know the real meaning of words like *never* and *always*. She hadn't known how devastating the one impulsive act of turning away could be. It meant that she could never take her place beside Fletcher again. Someone else had filled it. The realization made her heart wrench with pain, and perversely she hated him even more for not making her see the truth. But perhaps he hadn't known either. If only he hadn't pushed her to the edge with his accusation about Steve that night. If only he had cared just a little more, there might have been hope.

Blinking back stinging tears, Casey stiffened and took a long, faltering breath. She had to stop the useless memories. If she had learned anything at all the past couple of years, it was that she could survive only by not giving in to sentiment.

When she felt a gentle hand on her shoulder, Casey knew that it was Fletcher's.

"I didn't mean to hurt you, Casey," he whispered.

She shivered at his warm breath in her ear. "Really? I think that's exactly what you intended to do, Fletcher. I think you came here specifically to make a fool of me."

"Then you missed the whole point." His hand slid down her back and away. He stepped to her side and shoved his hands into the pockets of his trousers. "We just don't sail the same seas, do we?"

"No, I suppose not." Her gaze fastened on a luminous fish that hovered near a clump of seaweed.

"We'll talk later, Casey. At home." He looked at his watch and then at her. "Priscilla and I will leave now and let you and Steve have your evening together."

"That's kind of you. Especially since there isn't much of the evening left to salvage." Biting sarcasm was her only defense against his compassionate tone. She could stand anything but his sympathy.

Casey remained at the aquarium until she saw the door close behind Fletcher and Priscilla. When she returned to the table one glance at Steve told her that his pleasant mood had been replaced by one of trouble and confusion. And it was all her fault. The carefree evening she had planned had been shattered by the sparks that ignited between her and Fletcher.

"Steve, this can't have been the most inspiring evening you've ever had," she apologized.

"Well, maybe not inspiring, but certainly enlightening." He smiled and patted her hand. "You're still in love with him, aren't you?"

Casey swallowed hard before she nodded. "Yes."

"And I was the biggest fool two years ago." He shook his head and drummed his fingers on the table. "Casey, you must know I was in love with you."

Casey's eyes went wide for a moment. Then she slapped at him playfully. "Don't be silly, Steve."

"Oh, I was silly, all right," he continued. "I gave you every hint that's decent to give a married woman, but you were so much in love with Fletcher that you were blind to it all."

"Oh, sure." She leaned back in her chair and folded her

arms across her breasts. "Now tell me the one about looking from afar." She smiled skeptically.

"You don't know how true that is, Casey." Steve's voice softened to a whisper. "I got as close as I dared, but Fletcher wasn't blind. He knew how I felt about you."

She stared into Steve's brown eyes and suddenly knew that he was serious. "Apparently, Fletcher thought I felt the same way about you." Casey sipped her coffee, then set it aside. "He never gave me a chance to explain why you were there that night."

"I know." Steve nodded. "As your doctor, I couldn't explain, either, except to deny that there was anything going on between us—not on your part, anyway. But Casey, don't you think you should tell him now?"

She shook her head and sighed. "That was just one of the problems between us, Steve. I'm afraid there's no way to explain all of them away."

He rose and took her hand, then pulled her from the chair. "Go home and try, Casey. I have a feeling Fletcher is ready to talk."

When Steve paid the check and walked her to the Scout, Casey said good-bye and kissed his cheek. Steve was probably right, she thought, switching on the motor. Fletcher would want to talk, but what was really left to say? Perhaps he wouldn't want her to stay until the well came in. He might want her to leave immediately.

Fear of a final showdown kept her driving around for what seemed like hours. When she finally did return to the ranch Casey stood at the heavy oak door and prepared herself for anything Fletcher might say. If she could just get through the next few minutes without showing the hurt and pain she felt, she would be home free.

How ironic, she thought. Free to return to Dallas and wallow in misery. Free to live the rest of her life alone. That's what freedom meant.

She hid her surprise when Fletcher opened the door and stood to let her pass.

"Come in, Casey." His blond hair was disheveled, and the tiny lines around his eyes seemed etched in stone.

She summoned every ounce of courage within her and steeled herself against the determined look in his eyes. Walking into the living room, she sat on the china-blue easy chair, the only place that would give her strength.

"Would you like me to leave, Fletcher?"

"No. Let *me* do the honors this time." His smile was scornful as he walked to the bar and almost flung the ice cubes into a glass. "Get up, Casey."

"I'd rather sit if you don't mind." Her thoughts raced with confusion. She had never seen Fletcher in such a distraught state.

"Get up. You're not holding court tonight." In two strides he stood before her and took her by the shoulders. Lifting her from the chair, he stayed long enough to see that she would, indeed, stand, then turned and walked back to the bar. "Before I leave, you're going to hear a few home truths." He downed one drink, then began mixing another.

"Fletcher, I don't want to—" She stopped in midsentence as he crossed the room again and gripped her arm tightly.

"You know, they used to call you the Ice Queen in college. Don't pull away," he commanded when she stiffened. "There were other names, too. *Cast Iron Casey* was one. You needed no one and nothing to make your life complete. No one could pierce your armor. Like a fool, I thought I had done just that when you agreed to marry me. I was sure it was all a facade, but I decided to treat you just the way you seemed to want to be treated."

"Fletcher, don't." Her throat was dry and she trembled inside.

He held up his glass and shook his head. "No, let me continue with this touching confession. You see, Casey, I didn't want to push my way into your life, where I wasn't welcome—like your work, your personal feelings. So I stayed away."

"That wasn't the way it was, Fletcher." Her breasts heaved at the sound of his derisive chuckle. She gathered her thoughts into a thundercloud, rumbling and threatening to shoot bolts of lightning.

"Yes, Casey, that *is* the way it was. You told me not long ago that I never cared. Not true. Not true," he said, shaking his head slowly. "I wanted to kill Steve Howard that night I found you in his arms, but I didn't. I figured that would be the surest way to make you run like hell. I said nothing because I thought that was the only way to keep you, never making any demands, never telling you what *I* wanted. All you seemed to need was my encouragement to do whatever *you* wanted to do." He shrugged. "In the end, you ran anyway. Why, Casey?"

"You're drunk, Fletcher." She pushed at his chest, but he cupped her chin so that she could do nothing except look into his stormy eyes.

"No, I'm not—yet. But I intend to be before the night is over." He set his glass on a table beside the chair, then held her shoulders in his strong hands. "One of us is going to talk, Casey. Since you don't seem to have much to say, shall I continue?"

She lowered her gaze and knew that nothing would stop him from telling her all the things she didn't want to hear.

"Let's see, now. Where were we? Oh, yes. You left me, and I waited two years, hoping you'd return."

"Stop it!" She flung his hands away, unable to check the anger that exploded inside her. "You weren't idle all that time. Priscilla is proof of that."

"Priscilla. Maybe I haven't been fair with her." He

frowned and looked away. "She's been honest in her love for me, but I—"

"Honest?" Casey brushed past him and stepped to the bar. "That's not a word I'd use to describe her, but then you must know her better than I do. Why don't you go to her now?" Pouring herself a glass of whiskey, she prayed it would stop the throbbing at her temples.

"Maybe I should settle for her. At least she decides what she wants, based on feelings. Unlike you, who insists on cold, calculating reason to guide you."

She sipped her drink and ignored the stinging in her throat. "At one time you would have called her cloying and insipid, Fletcher."

"Being honest about feelings is not weak." He leaned across the bar until his warm breath fanned her face. "Try it sometime."

Thoughts ricocheted through her mind as she debated. No, it was too risky, too painful. "What good would it do?" she asked quietly. "People only get hurt when they wear their hearts on their sleeves."

He stared at her for a moment before his shoulders sagged. The light flickered and extinguished in his eyes before he turned away. The sneer in his voice cut to her soul. "Now, that's a statement I should've expected from you. I asked you to come back—"

"I know why you sent for me. And it makes a mockery of almost everything you've said. You wanted the land because it may contain oil." She saw his back stiffen before he turned toward her. The shock in his eyes gave her the courage and contempt she needed to go on. "You were willing to do whatever you had to do to get my property. That included making love to me when you didn't really care at all." Her own words as mere thoughts had hurt but, spoken, they carried the force of piercing arrows

169

through her heart. "Well, you'll get the land you schemed for. Now, tell me who's cold and calculating."

Nothing prepared her for the rage that darkened his eyes. The entire room seemed to fill with the clenching and unclenching of his fists. She stepped backward, truly afraid of the blistering silence. Pain, pure hatred, showed in his every movement as he slammed around the bar toward her. She molded herself to the wall, but he found her and jerked her to stand in front of him. She didn't dare look away. Big hands wrapped around her small wrists, and Casey realized with shocking awareness that Fletcher had never—never *before*—touched her in such fury. When he did so now, she shrank from him like a wounded animal, but he yanked her forward again.

"You— Oh, you bitch!" His whole body shuddered with the words. "You're wrong. Do you hear me? You're wrong!"

"Fletcher, I—"

"Shut up!" Then, staring down at the trembling hands he held, Fletcher closed his eyes. "Oh, my God." Without warning he flung her away and clutched a glass on the bar. "Why did I ever bring you back here? You don't trust anyone. You'll never change." His palm swept his face with a grating rub. She stared in wonder at this man she didn't know as he paced with the fierce compulsion of a predator. "I'll leave in the morning," he said, his chest heaving. "I'll stay away until you've gone."

"You don't have to—" The piercing shatter of glass against the opposite wall made her draw back in terror.

"I do!" he shouted. "I *do* have to! Do you think I could stay here with you?" He shook his head, his voice quivering, low. "No." She cringed at the defeat in his eyes. When she saw him moving away from her, she wanted to reach out, but the chill of his words pinned her arms to her sides. "Just one more thing," he said, his back rigid, his palm pressed hard against the doorjamb. "When you go back to Dallas you might want to look over our divorce settlement. A little light reading to keep you warm on cold nights—Cactus Rose." Fletcher walked from the room.

Her body and mind gave way to the crushing knowledge that perhaps she had seen him for the last time. All energy drained from her as she sank to a chair.

Cactus Rose, she thought. Why did it hurt so much when Fletcher said it? She had never wanted him to know the humiliating label bestowed on her by men who could never understand her as she thought Fletcher had. It didn't matter where he had heard the term. The fact that he believed it was paramount, though, and made her wince with pain. He thought her incapable of love, incapable of sharing. Perhaps he thought she was incapable of any feelings at all.

Inadvertently she stared at a fixed spot on the hardwood floor and turned over in her mind the mass of accusations and observations he had made. She sat until all his statements piled to a jumbled heap in her mind, until her limbs were stiff with tension. Still, no clear course of action presented itself. She longed for logic and reason to return and take the feeling of utter destruction away.

When she switched off the lights and made her way upstairs to the sitting room, Casey sat on the window seat and gathered her knees to her breasts. She knew sleep wouldn't come easily this night. Bits and pieces of her life with Fletcher drifted through her mind until it became clear how he had come to his conclusions. From his point of view and contrary to all her previous beliefs, she supposed *she* must have been the one who pushed *him* away by her own insecurities, her own fear of letting him see her need for him.

As she looked to the east and waited for the sun to give the first reflections of daybreak, Casey was aware of a

CHAPTER TEN

"Oil at 5,025 feet." Casey penned her final entry in the log before she closed the folder and laid it aside. A yawn escaped her as she rose from her camp chair to stretch muscles that begged for rest after the long, sleepless night at the well site.

The hiss of a hydraulic lift temporarily drowned out the noise of the rumbling engines, and Casey watched the portable derrick being laid to rest on its side. In the cool morning sunlight roughnecks, spurred by the promise of sleep, gathered heavy equipment and tools for storage in the doghouse behind her.

"Well, Casey, you were right on the money," the drilling foreman said as he stepped to her side. "To be honest, Mr. Ames thought we'd have to drill a lot deeper."

"I know, Dave." Casey smiled at his steel-toed work boots, then lifted her gaze to blue eyes that squinted respect. "Until I saw the core samples yesterday, I was beginning to have a few doubts myself."

Dave laughed as he raised a denim shirt-sleeve to wipe the streaks of grime from his weatherworn face. "You made a believer out of Mr. Ames, though. I wouldn't be surprised if he asks you to stay on."

"Maybe," Casey said, remembering Henry's pat on the back earlier that morning.

"This looks like a good-size field," Dave continued. "I'll look forward to working with you on the next well."

"Thanks, but my work's finished here, Dave. I'll be going home tomorrow."

"Too bad. We'll miss you."

His sincere tone prompted Casey to extend her hand. "I'll miss you, too."

He shook her hand and said good-bye, then turned away to shout more orders to his crew.

As Casey gathered the logs and stowed them in the Scout, she looked up to see Mack's two-tone pickup bouncing across the pasture toward her. As he pulled the truck to a halt beside the Scout she felt his congratulations even before he slammed the door and greeted her with a bear hug.

"You did it, Casey!" he shouted, lifting her off the ground, then setting her down gently. "I just got the news a few minutes ago. Fletcher will be proud to know how well you handled this job."

"Have you heard from him, Mack?" she asked, hoping he wouldn't notice her eager anticipation.

His smile faded to a look of apology as he rubbed his woolly beard. "No, but he'll be proud, just the same. Maybe he'll be home in time for Henry's celebration to-night."

She lowered her gaze and shook her head. "No, Mack. I don't think so."

"Look, you're tired." Mack reached out to lift her chin. "You need some rest and some food. Let's go home, and I'll have Ella cook two steaks with redeye gravy. Now, how does that sound?"

It sounded awful, but Casey's lips curved to a hollow smile anyway. "I'm ready whenever you are."

"Good. By the way, a letter came for you just before I left the ranch." He reached into his back pocket and presented her with a slightly crumpled white envelope. "It looks kind of important."

Casey focused on the return address and knew that her attorney had finally sent the requested copy of her divorce settlement. Perhaps now she could lay to rest at least one of the doubts Fletcher had introduced to plague her conscience.

"Go ahead and open it, if you like. I've got time," Mack stated as nonchalantly as his curiosity would allow.

"It can wait, Mack." She smiled at his shrug of indifference, then seated herself behind the wheel of the Scout. Before she switched on the key Casey turned for one last look at the well. Success would have been so much sweeter, she thought, had Fletcher been there to share in the fruits of her labors on his behalf. She closed her eyes and let the loneliness settle over her again, a feeling that rarely left her these days. With a wave to the crew she followed Mack's truck through the pasture and bump gate, then turned onto the winding dirt road.

The morning sun had already begun to heat up the countryside, and Casey longed for a cool bath and bed. Most of all, though, she was eager to look over the divorce papers. She remembered the night, that last night, when Fletcher had suggested she might want to read them again. She had no wish to rehash a dead issue, but his sarcastic remark had piqued her curiosity a little more each day until, finally, she had phoned her attorney for a copy.

Upon her arrival at the ranch Casey went straight to the study and placed the well logs on the oak desk. Then she sat in Fletcher's roomy leather chair and ripped open the long envelope. A quick scan of the legal papers brought no startling information, so Casey forced her mind to slow down and read the words more carefully. The legal phrases were sometimes difficult, although not impossible to understand. When she had finished she dropped the pages onto the desk and leaned back in the chair.

Where were the revelations? she wondered, wrinkling her nose. The settlement was very simple. She got six hundred forty acres of land. Period.

Casey swiveled the chair for a look out the window toward the stables. A sombrero-clad boy curried Marengo while Cinder snorted and nervously paced the paddock's perimeter, as if impatient to have his mate's grooming over and done. Casey smiled wryly. Cinder had exhibited that same insensitivity the day of the picnic, she thought. The day that Fletcher had shown her the land for the first time. The memory of his scheme to regain control of the land paled beside her love for him. The shock that had pinched his face as he denied her accusation still haunted her, still nagged at her heart until she was left staring into darkness long into the lonely nights.

She turned back to the desk to hold the papers in her hands again. Although the black print represented a legal parting of the ways, it was her only connection with Fletcher now.

"Ella's got the steaks on," Mack announced as he entered the room and seated himself in a chair opposite Casey. Puffing on a thick cigar, he raised his feet to rest on the desk and eyed her thoughtfully. "You look dog tired, Casey. Hit the sack right after breakfast, so you'll be rested for the party tonight."

"I think I'll skip the celebration, Mack."

"That just won't get it, Casey," he said gruffly. "Henry's expecting you there, and I think you should make an appearance."

She smiled at his moping frown. "Since when do you care about appearances, Mack?"

"Well, never, but Henry has something to talk over with you, and I promised I'd—"

"Deliver?" she prompted with a sideways glance. "Okay. I'll go for a few minutes, but Mack, when are you going to stop interfering? I thought when you were caught intercepting my calls from Steve, you'd—"

"Well, I'm glad we got that settled," he said, peering at the papers on the desk. "What are you reading there?"

Taking a deep breath, she sighed and shook her head. "A copy of my divorce settlement. I've read it over and over, but I just can't figure it out."

Mack swung his feet to the floor and leaned forward. "Well, I've read *War and Peace*. Let me take a look at it."

With resignation she slid the document to rest in front of him and watched his discerning gaze travel down each of the two pages. Then he looked up at her.

"Looks short and sweet to me. What is it you don't understand?"

"I think I understand it all, but before Fletcher—left, he suggested I examine it again. He hinted that I might've overlooked something."

"Hmmm." Mack frowned and tapped his cigar against the edge of an ashtray. "Everything seems okay. Did he give you the deed to the acreage?"

"Yes. It's in my safety deposit box in Dallas."

"And you didn't get any mineral rights, so there's no mineral deed to worry about."

"Mineral deed? I don't remember . . ." Her words trailed off as she felt the blood drain from her face. "Oh, Mack! What have I done?"

"What is it, Casey? What's wrong?" He walked to her side and perched on the edge of the desk.

177

"I don't own the mineral rights." Her heart pounded at the realization.

"I know." Mack shrugged. "Fletcher and I do."

She pushed herself up from the chair, regret permeating her thoughts. "He'll never forgive me for the things I said."

"That's ridiculous. Of course he will," Mack insisted. "But what did you say?"

Casey brushed past him and stepped to the bookshelves that lined one paneled wall. "I thought Fletcher wanted the land for the oil that might be on it, Mack. I didn't realize the oil already belonged to him."

"You're a geologist, Casey. You should've known that mineral rights don't automatically go with the land."

"I know. I know." She closed her eyes and sank onto the overstuffed chair that Mack had vacated. "But at the time of the divorce, I didn't know which way was up. I filed all the papers away and never looked at them again. It was too—" She stopped and ran slender fingers through her hair, then dropped her hand to the arm of the chair. The muscles in her throat constricted, but Casey felt compelled to go on. "When Fletcher confessed how he felt all the time we were married, I didn't believe him. Instead, I slapped him in the face with silly accusations about the land. He was right, Mack. We just don't sail the same seas."

"Oh, I don't believe that." Mack's smile was compassionate as he came to her side and squeezed her shoulder affectionately. "I think you and Fletcher have the same destination in mind, Casey. It's the course you follow that rocks the boat. You just need to decide who's to navigate and who's to steer. That's all. I'm sure when Fletcher comes back, he'll—"

"He won't, Mack." The words wrenched from her heart

as she rose and walked to the door. "He'll stay away until I'm gone, and I can't say that I blame him."

Casey touched the ivory ankh at her throat and sipped the champagne that Henry had put in her hand. Soft melodic music drifted indoors from the terrace to mingle with the sound of tinkling crystal. Casual conversations blended together all around her, and Casey smiled at her own discordant thoughts. Although most of the guests in Henry's spacious, split-level home were old friends of hers and Fletcher's, Casey felt out of place without Fletcher at her side to inject his own brand of wit and charm. She decided to stay a few more minutes, then slip quietly back to the ranch. There was still her packing to finish, and she had hardly slept at all that day.

Stifling a yawn, she looked up, mildly surprised to see Priscilla clinging to Tom Weston, a longtime Circle R foreman of the Santa Rosa division. A tall, muscular man with curly dark hair, he was obviously enjoying his status as Priscilla's escort, but Casey couldn't smother a frown at the excessive attention Priscilla paid him while Fletcher was away. And Tom should have better sense, Casey thought, setting her drink on the cherrywood table behind her. She let her emerald gaze search the room for Mack, but before she could track his silver-streaked hair Henry touched her arm.

"Would you come to my office, Casey, so we can talk privately?"

"Of course, Henry," she replied, aware of the recent change in his attitude. "I really shouldn't stay much longer, though."

He led the way to a large room elegantly decorated with polished mahogany furniture. When he motioned her to a chair, she obeyed, glancing at the thick books that filled the shelves of three walls. Books on the petroleum industry, no doubt, she noted, as Henry closed the door and took the seat behind his cluttered desk.

"What can I do for you, Henry?" she asked, eager to get to the heart of the matter.

"Well, you could agree to stay and help develop the new oil field, for one thing." He smoothed his balding head, then rested his arms on the desk. "Before you say anything let me tell you that, although I was a pompous idiot when we first met, I've come to respect your ability. I should've listened to Fletcher, but—"

"Enough said, Henry," Casey interrupted with a chuckle. "I appreciate your offer, but I really can't accept. My own company has assignments waiting for me."

"Can't you work something out with your partners? You see, I'd like to retain your firm on a permanent basis, with the understanding that *you* will handle my account. You wouldn't be working in a strictly geological capacity, but it would give you a chance to broaden your knowledge of the oil industry."

"It all sounds very attractive, but are you sure all your partners share your high opinion of me?"

Henry rose from his chair and walked to the window. "If you're referring to my daughter, I know I've made some mistakes with her, but I'm confident they can be rectified. From now on I'll see that she takes a more active interest in the business, or she'll find herself another one. She's been entirely too dependent on me, and it's got to stop."

"I'm sure Fletcher will take care of that." The words were difficult to say, but Casey swallowed hard and continued. "When they're—married. . . ."

"Married?" Henry chuckled as he turned toward her. "Fletcher won't marry Priscilla. She made a big mistake, giving him that ultimatum."

180

Casey felt her stomach stir with apprehension. "What kind of ultimatum?"

"Not long ago she demanded that he announce their engagement or she planned to find someone else."

"What—what did Fletcher say to that?"

Henry shrugged and looked away as if deep in thought. "He said he couldn't marry her. I suppose you noticed her out there sidling up to Tom Weston."

"When—when did all this happen?" Casey asked, her throat dry with a need to know.

"The final showdown came during the trip to San Antonio, I guess. Priscilla was a little upset the night you—I mean Fletcher—got into that disagreement at the bar."

The memory seized her and left her weak with remorse. The air in the room seemed nonexistent as Casey rose from the chair and forced control to her voice. "Henry, I'll let you know about the job. Tell Mack—tell Mack I'll see him at the ranch. I have to leave now." Fletcher really had loved her, and she had refused to trust him. Now . . . she had to find him.

"But Casey—"

"Good night, Henry." Without looking back she crossed the room and opened the door.

She caught her breath at the sight of Fletcher in a light-gray suit, his fist poised to knock. As his hand lowered slowly to his side, her lips parted to speak, but no words would come. Starved for the sight of him, she let her gaze devour his tall, powerful body. Her eyes drank in his thick blond hair, his firm, yet somehow gentle lips above his cleft chin, the faint scar that shadowed his cheek, and his passionate, blue-gray eyes—eyes that stirred the yearning deep within her and drew it to the surface until every atom in her body cried for his touch.

"Take me home, Fletcher. Please."

With comforting acquiescence his fingers reached out to

stroke her cheek, then softly traced her full lips. Closing her eyes, she covered his hand with hers and kissed his palm.

"Well, Fletcher!" Henry called from behind her. "I'm so glad you could make it tonight."

She stared up at Fletcher, her eyes begging him to get rid of Henry and anyone else who might take the magic of the moment away. A soft smile curved his lips and wrapped her in a blanket of anticipation. His hand slid around her waist and drew her to his side.

For the next few minutes Casey was vaguely aware of the guests greeting Fletcher, but her whole being concentrated on the future, when she could be alone with him. Each time her knees threatened to give way at the maddening small talk, she felt Fletcher's supporting arm tighten around her, giving her strength to wait a little longer. She smiled in all the right places as he fielded any questions directed at her.

She remained in the glow of his protection all the way back to the ranch. As the car sped along under the star-studded sky his silence didn't seem strange at all, for she shared his unspoken need to begin the beginning at home in the room she had shared with him.

When she found herself walking up the wide steps beside him, he opened the massive door and led her across the threshold. His eyes bespoke a silent promise as he willed her up the stairs and into the bedroom, bathed in the soft glow of moonlight.

She slid trembling fingers around his **neck and** rested her cheek against his **hard** chest. Closing her eyes, she reveled in the rhythm of his heartbeat as he held her tightly.

"I love you, Casey. I always have."

His whispered words were so simple and, yet, they set

forth the tidal wave of love inside her. Tears stinging her eyes, she raised her face to his.

"Fletcher, what happened to us so long ago?"

"I don't know. I can hardly stand to think about the years that you weren't with me." His voice quivered with emotion as he gently cupped her chin. "Don't make me wait any longer. We need each other. What will it take to make you believe in me again? I know you did once, but—"

She raised a finger to touch his lips, then traced the firm line of his jaw. "I do believe in you. I love you. And if you can ever forgive me . . ."

His muffled "Shhh" against her hair as he gathered her to him bespoke much more than forgiveness. His hands caressed her back and then moved down to her hips. His demanding kisses stirred the embers of passion within her, leaving her breathless and aching for more. He reached round to unzip her dress, then slipped the material from her shoulders to reveal her breasts. His smoldering eyes and sensuous hands savored each part of her as he removed her bra and panties.

With a hunger born of desperate love denied too long, she freed him of his jacket and tie. By the time his shirt came away her fingers trembled fiercely. When she tried with little success to unbuckle his belt, Fletcher reached for her and held her to him, stroking her hair.

"Do you need help?" he asked gently.

She nuzzled against his hard chest. "Oh, Fletcher, I— need you." It was such a monumental release—to finally say it—to admit openly, unashamedly, her weakness for this man. Her eyes filled with tears as he pulled her completely into the realm of his love. Strengthened by his reassurance, she stepped back with renewed vigor for the matter at hand. Making quick work of the rest of his clothes, she tossed them to the floor. She wanted him. She would *have* him. Spreading her palms against his chest, she buried her fingers in the soft hair. They stood for several minutes exploring, tasting, touching, as though they were lovers possessing each other for the first time. But he was no stranger to her, nor she to him.

She was home again. Home with Fletcher and all the delicious, wonderful feelings that life with him would let her experience. His tantalizing kisses were just as exciting as before, his touch as devastating. But now she felt a delicious freedom, a new level in her love for him. She watched the moonlight play on the rugged features of his face, softened by her touch. Together they sank to the bed. She gave herself up to his arms gladly, with such tenderness for him.

"I'll never let you go again. Never," he whispered in a husky voice. "I need you always."

"And I need you." There was no hesitation, no doubt as she branded his mouth with eager kisses. With her tongue she teased his lips until he shivered, then crushed her to him. He caressed her lovingly in all the ways that had never failed to make her his own, his fingers exploring the delicious curves that yielded so completely to his touch.

Her lips moved over him, nibbling, savoring, fueling her own passion with his low moans of delight. She unlocked his soul and drove him to soaring heights of enchantment.

When she felt him quiver with need she moved onto him, her body singing, sharing with his. Knowing that he belonged to her and she to him, she made a silent vow to never again deny this man her love . . . a boundless love that could not be destroyed by elusive time or even the fallacious doubts magnified by her own imagination. She wrapped herself around him, moving with him as their mutual passion mounted to excruciating intensity. In rapturous exultation she clung to him, feeling the powerful life-force flow from his body to hers. She drew her strength from him and gave it back again. As he moaned softly, burying his face in the curve of her shoulder, she held him to her breasts. His tremolo sigh was her reaffirmation of his love, and she needed nothing more. But she would have more . . . a lifetime of more. The knowledge made her smile in adoration as she rolled to his side to snuggle against him. She lay in the circle of his embrace until their heartbeats returned to normal. Then she slipped out of bed to enjoy the starry night that greeted her at the window.

Loving thoughts drifted across her blissful mind. Thoughts that she longed to share with Fletcher. As if sensing her mood, he rose and slid his arms around her to cover her breasts. When his lips brushed her neck, she shivered.

"Cold?" he asked, drawing her closer.

"Warm," she corrected with a smile. "Very warm. I've been lonely without you, Fletcher. Where have you been?"

"Not far. I tried the beach house first, but that was no good. Then Susan and John's. Every place I went only reminded me of you. So I came back and bunked at Tom Weston's. When the well came in, I knew it was my last chance and I had to take it. I couldn't let you go without trying once more."

Casey pulled his arms tighter around her at this and snuggled against his chest. "Is that why you came to the party tonight?"

"Yes. You looked so beautiful that I had to touch you. Thank God you didn't turn away this time."

"I won't ever do that again, darling," she assured him. "I was such a fool to think you would ever deceive me. When Mack told me that you owned the mineral rights to the land, I felt so ashamed. And then when I learned that you weren't going to marry Priscilla . . ."

185

He stiffened and turned her to him, lifting her chin. "Why would I marry her when I'm in love with you?"

Her cheeks warmed with color as she lowered her gaze. "Fletcher, I was so jealous—you made love to *me* one night and took *her* to San Antonio the next day."

"Oh, Casey." He pushed the hair away from her face. "Is that why you were so cold to me?"

She took a deep breath and sighed. "I was hurt, Fletcher, and so humiliated."

His arms went around her again as he pulled her close. "I should've told you the truth from the beginning. I did mislead you. I wanted you back; so, when Mack agreed to drill for oil, it seemed the perfect excuse to get you here. I didn't think you'd stay for any other reason. Then I invested in John's boat so you wouldn't have to sell the land."

Casey pulled away slightly and frowned. "Did Susan tell you about that?"

"Yes," Fletcher replied with a chuckle. "She and Mack could co-anchor the ten o'clock news." Then a serious expression spread over his face. "There's one more thing about Priscilla that I need to clear up. She's been a good friend at times when I needed one badly. But there's been nothing more than companionship between us."

Her arms slid around his neck. Drawing his head close to hers, she nibbled tenderly on his ear. "In the future I'll make it *my* business to see that you get your share of companionship and more."

"Hmmm." His fingers teased her spine with soft, slow strokes. "Is Cactus Rose finally shedding all her prickly needles?"

She smiled and closed her eyes. "It's the least I can do for my desert prince."

186

LOOK FOR NEXT MONTH'S
CANDLELIGHT ECSTASY ROMANCES®

THE SEEDS OF SINGING
by Kay McGrath

To the primitive tribes of New Guinea, the
seeds of singing are the essence of courage.
To Michael Stanford and Catherine Morgan,
two young explorers on a lost expedition,
they symbolize a passion that defies war,
separation, and time itself. In the unmapped
highlands beyond the jungle, in a world
untouched since the dawn of time, Michael
and Catherine discover a passion men and
women everywhere only dream about, a love
that will outlast everything.

A DELL BOOK   19120-3 $3.95

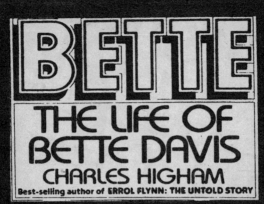